"Don't You Owe Me Something?"

He looked her over in a predatory way and Alison found herself shivering slightly

"Owe you some[...] incredulously. "[...] a thing."

"I think you do." His lips curled up in amusement and there were deep and mocking glints in his eyes.

"I want you out of my house," Alison said through clenched teeth.

"Not until I receive some payment," he responded, advancing toward her. "Payment for a nice evening."

And then Matt gathered her into his arms and pressed his lips to hers.

LAURA EDEN
currently makes her home outside of Washington, D.C., along with her husband, a Canadian diplomat, and their two daughters. *Mistaken Identity* is her first Silhouette Romance, and readers will be pleased to know that it will not be her last.

Dear Reader:

At Silhouette we try to publish books with you, our reader, in mind, and we're always trying to think of something new. We're very pleased to announce the creation of Silhouette First Love, a new line of contemporary romances written by the very finest young adult writers especially for our twelve-to-sixteen-year-old readers. First Love has many of the same elements you've enjoyed in Silhouette Romances—love stories, happy endings and the same attention to detail and description—but features heroines and situations with which our younger readers can more easily identify.

First Love from Silhouette will be available in bookstores this October. We will introduce First Love with six books, and each month thereafter we'll bring you two new First Love romances.

We welcome any suggestions or comments, and I invite you to write to us at the address below.

Karen Solem
Editor-in-Chief
Silhouette Books
P.O. Box 769
New York, N.Y. 10019

LAURA EDEN
Mistaken Identity

Silhouette *Romance*

Published by Silhouette Books New York

America's Publisher of Contemporary Romance

SILHOUETTE BOOKS, a Simon & Schuster Division of
GULF & WESTERN CORPORATION
1230 Avenue of the Americas, New York, N.Y. 10020

ISBN: 0-671-57105-2

First Silhouette printing September, 1981

10 9 8 7 6 5 4 3 2 1

Mistaken Identity

Chapter One

Alison Ramsey combed her ash-blond hair, which fell from a middle part to her shoulders, to form a smooth bell shape around her oval face. As she patted one final wandering strand into place, she gave a big sigh and then smiled ruefully at her image in the mirror. It was the last evening of her week's vacation in Key West, and, as she had all of her other evenings, she was going to spend it alone.

Which wasn't to say that she hadn't enjoyed her holiday, she reflected as she carefully applied mascara to her eyelashes and a pale pink lipstick to her lips. Being able to use George and Karen's apartment had been great, and all the neighbors she had met at the condominium poolside had been very pleasant. Mr. Daniels, a charming octogenarian, had played a tough game of rummy, and Oliver Briscome, a gentlemanly widower of about seventy, had even hinted that there was still some life left in the old boy yet. And hadn't she really needed a rest after her hectic—and successful—campaign for a position on the town council?

Still, Alison thought as she heaved another sigh, she'd had enough of peace and quiet. And while she wasn't the type to go to a singles bar or a disco until all hours of the morning, she was definitely restless. When she had awakened this morning to a bright stream of sunshine pouring into her bedroom window, she had quailed at the idea of another day sunbathing by the pool or on the beach. Then an idea had struck her, and she had thrown aside the bedcovers with an excited hand. Tonight she would mark the end of her vacation with a luxurious and extravagant flourish—a grand finale Alison Ramsey–style!

She had spent the day shopping for the perfect dress and had found it in a tiny boutique hidden among the souvenir shops. The blue silk matched the aquamarine of her eyes, and the cut emphasized her willowy height and slender curves. It had a mandarin collar, a sleeveless bodice that buttoned down to her waist with tiny silk-covered buttons and loops, a matching sash belt, and a form-fitting skirt with a slit up one side. The salesgirl had murmured admiringly when Alison had tugged on her white high heels and revolved slowly in the boutique's three-way mirror.

The price of the dress had taken her breath away, and its seductive lines had almost undermined her courage. When she walked in it, the high slit in the skirt revealed glimpses of her long, tanned legs and the silk fabric clung to her every curve. It made her look alluring and provocative, but at the same time its cost would reduce her to brown-bag lunches for weeks. Alison had taken out her wallet with determination. Grand gestures, after all, called for superlative clothes.

She patted a slight dusting of powder onto her nose, thankful that her smooth complexion had tanned so well that she barely needed any makeup. The Florida sun had put a glow into her cheeks that served to highlight the blue-green of her eyes and her white-blond hair. As she slung her white evening bag over one shoulder, she took a last look in the mirror. The effect was perfect, Alison thought. She looked just like the type of sophisticated woman who had enough *savoir-faire* and glamor to dine alone at Key West's most exclusive and expensive restaurant, the Hotel Amérique's Pavillon Française.

The hotel's foyer was richly decorated with red oriental carpets, plush red velvet couches and several large cut-glass chandeliers. Elegantly dressed men and women passed Alison by as she stood hesitantly in the middle of the lobby. Her earlier determination was failing her as she looked toward the Pavillon Française's impressive and ornate wrought-iron doorway. The dinner was going to cost her a small fortune, and even the most excellent food wasn't going to camouflage the fact that she was dining alone without a friend or companion. Only the fact that she had made a reservation that afternoon kept Alison from a quick exit and a search for a less costly and less formal meal.

With a deep breath she pushed open the heavy door and walked into the Pavillon Française's dimly lit entrance. The faint scent of roses assailed her nose, and she blinked slightly as her eyes adjusted to the soft lighting. Darkness had not yet fallen outside the hotel's front doors, but inside the restaurant it was already nighttime. The result was an atmosphere of luxury and discretion.

The room was decorated in blues and gold, and the silent waiters wore tuxedos of indigo. Each table, isolated from the others by strategically placed ferns and large plants, had a royal-blue tablecloth, gold-rimmed white china, and a floral decoration of roses in gleaming silver vases. The thick pale blue carpet absorbed the sounds of clinking silverware and glasses, and only the faint murmurings of voices came to Alison's ears.

"Ah, mademoiselle, we have been waiting for you." A heavily accented French voice spoke beside her, and Alison turned to see the maître d' at her left.

Waiting for her? How could they be waiting for her, when she hadn't given them her name yet? How could they know that she was the Alison Ramsey who had made a reservation that afternoon? She was about to say something when the maître d' took her firmly by the

9

elbow and led her into the dining room. "A table is ready. This way, please."

With a polite flourish he pulled out a blue velvet wing chair at a table that stood snugly in one corner, far from the eyes of other guests and shielded by a pot of delicately drooping ferns. Alison, in wordless confusion, automatically sat down, staring into his smiling face. "*Bon appétit,* mademoiselle," he said and then walked away. He was already long gone by the time Alison noticed that the table was set for two.

Alison frowned at the second place setting. Obviously the maître d' had confused her with someone else. Another woman in a blue dress, perhaps? And Alison could not help but wonder about the reaction of her proposed dinner companion. Would he or she be irate to discover that the table was already taken? Surely whoever it was would be polite enough to accept her explanation and graciously find another place.

The arrival of the menu drew Alison's attention away from the problem of her mistaken identity. As she glanced down the price list her eyes widened in shock. She had expected that the Pavillon would be expensive, but not that an entrée might approximate the national debt. Make that brown-bag lunches for months instead of weeks, she thought with chagrin. This grand finale for her vacation was going to leave her with a somewhat less than grand bank balance. She was concentrating so hard on the menu that she barely noticed the arrival of a waiter. He placed a glass of white wine at her elbow and then glided away before Alison had a chance to stop him.

Alison was partial to white wine. She picked up the glass and tasted the drink. Very dry, very nice. Whoever was supposed to be at this table had good taste, she decided approvingly. She turned back to the menu, sipping at her drink. The alcohol warmed her veins and supplied her with extra fortitude. Every dish sounded delicious, and after all, if she was going to throw financial caution to the winds, she might as well indulge in the most outrageous culinary delights.

Alison was trying to choose between Crab Glori-anne, described as "a dish of tender Florida crab broiled in a delicate sauce of mushrooms and spices," or Pompano à la Floridienne, a local fish baked with butter and fine herbs, when the same quiet waiter removed her empty glass, replaced it with another, and placed a dish of hot escargot swimming in butter sauce before her.

Alison sat in speechless astonishment as this transaction took place. Despite the wine, she knew perfectly well that she hadn't ordered a second glass—or the appetizer. In fact, she hadn't even ordered the *first* glass of wine, if it came to that. But she was far too intimidated by the elegance of her surroundings and the formality of the waiter to tell him that there must have been a mistake.

She nibbled on the end of one perfectly manicured gleaming pink nail, and a line appeared between her eyebrows. A glance down the list of hors d'oeuvres revealed that the price of escargots would feed her for several days back home. She mentally reviewed the contents of her wallet. She had thought she would have enough money for dinner *and* her return fare. Maybe the airport would have a bank that would be willing to cash a New York check? Maybe she would eat only the appetizer and cut out the entrée? Alison giggled slightly. Maybe the Pavillon Française needed another dishwasher?

"Over here, monsieur."

The voice of the maître d' broke into Alison's thoughts and she lowered the menu. A pair of dark brown eyes were making a slow inventory of her face, her neck, and lower, to where the silk of her dress outlined the curve of her breasts. Alison flushed and cleared her throat. She was about to launch into a long and detailed explanation of her presence when the

11

maître d', who was hovering at the stranger's elbow, pulled out the other chair with an even more polite and grand flourish than he had bestowed on Alison.

"Monsieur, your chair."

To Alison's total confusion, the tall, dark stranger sat down opposite her.

"Bon appétit, monsieur."

"Thank you, Henri." The stranger turned to Alison with an imperturbable expression. "I hope you've enjoyed your drink and escargots," he said. "I'm sorry that I'm late."

"Late?" she asked breathlessly.

"Yes, a slight . . . er, business disagreement, you might say."

The stranger turned and beckoned to a waiter, giving Alison a moment to collect her wits. Obviously, he had not noticed that she was the wrong woman. Was it possible that he and the woman who was supposed to be his dining companion were strangers to each other? Could this be a blind date? Did men make blind dates for dinners at expensive restaurants like the Pavillon? Alison supposed that they did, if they were wealthy enough. She glanced at him as he spoke to the waiter. His dark blue blazer sat impeccably on his broad shoulders, and his dark brown hair had been cut perfectly so that its thick waves curved in a stylish line over his ears and down his muscular neck. She had to admit that, whoever he was, he looked as if he could afford the Pavillon.

The man turned back to her and smiled. His teeth were very white in his lean, tanned face. He had thick, dark eyebrows over his deep-set brown eyes, a straight, aquiline nose, and full, curving lips. He was, Alison estimated, in his mid-thirties, and he was easily, she judged, the most handsome man she had ever seen.

"Are you enjoying your holiday here, Miss . . . Miss . . . ?"

Alison, surprised that he had known that she was

vacationing here, unwittingly supplied her name. "Ramsey . . . Alison Ramsey." Then, believing that the revelation of her name would give the game away, she steeled herself for an explosion, but the stranger didn't bat an eye. Although she kept her expression impassive, Alison was starting to get the odd feeling that she was involved in some strange spy plot, the kind that she had seen on television.

"And your holiday?" The stranger picked up the glass of Scotch that the waiter placed before him.

Alison narrowed her eyes slightly and decided to play his game. "I've had a wonderful time, Mr. . . . Mr. . . . ?" She gave him an inquisitive look. To her astonishment, Alison discovered that she was enjoying herself. Shame on you, Alison Ramsey, she chided herself. Whatever are you doing?

The stranger choked slightly on his drink. "Matt . . . er, Matt Edwards."

"You know, Mr. Edwards, I think we've met before." Alison watched him carefully for any sign that he was aware that their meeting was taking place under false pretenses.

He put down his glass, picked up the linen napkin, and placed it on his knees. "I don't think so, Miss Ramsey," he answered nonchalantly. "Where would we have met?"

Blast him. Now she was in a spot. "In Fairfax, New York," she said desperately, naming the first place that came to her mind, her own hometown.

Matt Edwards looked at her quizzically. "I've been there," he acknowledged, "but I don't think I ever met you there."

"You've been there?" Alison was nonplused. Fairfax was so small that she thought she knew every person who had ever passed through.

"Once." His answer was curt.

"Are you ready to order?" The waiter had come and was standing patiently by their table.

"Have you chosen, Miss Ramsey?"

Alison opened her menu and hesitated. In her encounter with the mysterious Matt Edwards she had totally forgotten her dilemma over the meal prices.

"Perhaps I should order for you, Miss Ramsey. I know the chef very well."

Alison took a deep breath and decided that now was the time to confess all to Matt Edwards and throw herself on his mercy. "Mr. Edwards . . ." she began, and then her resolve weakened.

Matt, noticing her reluctance, mistook it as indecision. "I'm sure you'll enjoy the lobster, Miss Ramsey," he broke in smoothly and proceeded to give the waiter their dinner order.

Alison was caught in a welter of emotions. She was astonished at her own behavior and the realization that she was enjoying the charade. It was deceitful, and yet, as far as she could see, it was harmless. After all, once dinner was over and she had paid her bill, she and this handsome stranger would merely go their separate ways. She would have had a pleasant and memorable evening, and the only person who would suffer shock would be her bank manager.

What she couldn't figure out were Matt Edwards' motives. It was surely odd that he knew neither the face nor the name of the woman with whom he had planned to dine. Of course, he had known that she was on vacation, Alison reminded herself and then quickly corrected that idea. No, he knew that the woman he was supposed to meet was on vacation. It was that simple.

Suddenly an unpleasant thought struck her. What would happen if the other woman, the right one, showed up now? That would cause a horrible, embarrassing scene. Alison glanced toward the restaurant's door, which remained steadfastly closed, and then looked up to see Matt Edwards surveying her face, one dark eyebrow arched. "Is anything the matter, Miss Ramsey?"

Alison's intention to tell the truth, and nothing but the truth, now disappeared completely under his amused glance. "Of course not," she said with asperity and began to eat her escargots.

For the rest of the meal, Matt Edwards seemed determined to pursue only lighthearted, impersonal topics. He asked about her stay in the Keys. Had she gone snorkeling off the reef? Boating in the ocean? Had she enjoyed the beaches? Alison regaled him with her experiences, making him laugh. She told him about the pelican that stole her lunch, and about the large whelk shell that she had found and thought to bring home, only to discover that it was inhabited by an enormous and very irate hermit crab.

The waiter came and went bearing trays of delicious food. Alison discovered that she was enjoying not only the meal but also her dining companion, who was relaxed, witty, and charming. Although she had never lacked for dates, Alison hadn't yet met a man she could consider more than a friend or companion. Matt Edwards was . . . different, she thought, watching him as he poured her another glass of wine. With a sense of regret, she realized that after this evening she would never see him again.

Intent on their dinner and their conversation, both Alison and Matt Edwards failed to notice a confrontation that took place at the Pavillon's entrance. A tall blond woman in a blue dress entered the restaurant and was greeted by the maître d'. To her questions, he shook his head. She argued, stamped her feet, and waved an angry fist in his face, but the maître d' vehemently refused to do whatever she was requesting. Finally, in defeat, she left, an angry look in her eyes.

A short time later, as Matt was telling Alison an amusing anecdote about an enormous horseshoe crab that he had encountered while scuba diving in the coral reef that surrounded Key West, the waiter arrived with a telephone.

"A call for you, monsieur." He plugged the phone into a jack beside the table.

"Please excuse me," Matt said, picking up the receiver.

"Of course," Alison answered and concentrated on extracting some lobster meat from a stubborn claw.

"How interesting," Matt Edwards was saying into the phone as Alison successfully speared the lobster and dipped it into the butter sauce. "How very interesting. Well, thanks for the information . . . right."

When he hung up, Alison smiled at him. "Business?" she asked.

"Monkey business, I think," he said, smiling back, but his eyes were cold, dark chips that held no amusement at all.

Alison, who was busy trying to garner another piece of lobster, continued blithely, "What sort of business are you in, Mr. Edwards?"

"Why don't you call me Matt?" he said silkily. "And if you don't mind, may I call you Alison?"

Alison nodded and sipped her wine. She had lost track of how many glasses she had drunk, but she wasn't letting that bother her in the least. After all, wasn't it the last night of her vacation, and wasn't she doing it up in style? She thought how silly she had been to be intimidated by this lovely and friendly restaurant. And the food was so good. Just wait until George and Karen heard about her adventure. Surely this was more exciting than a story about Mr. Daniels' rummy game or Oliver Briscome's little gallantries. Beaming with good cheer, Alison failed to notice that Matt Edwards had smoothly evaded her question or that his dark eyes, which were taking in her happy, flushed face, held a more curious and predatory expression than she would have liked.

"So, Alison, what do you do in the lovely little town of Fairfax?"

The wine had loosened Alison's tongue. Whereas earlier she had regretted telling this stranger her name, now she happily confided the details of her life: about growing up in a small town, her parents' retirement to Arizona, her job at the radio station that George owned, and her recent hard-fought election to the town council.

"What was the issue of your campaign?"

"Rezoning an old farm property."

"Let me guess," Matt said pleasantly. "Some firm wants to come in and commercialize it."

"They don't want to come in! They've already managed a sneaky deal with the farmer. They're a hotel-management firm, and they want to build a resort on the property."

Matt looked at the fire that sparked in Alison's wide aquamarine eyes. "And I take it you are against the scheme," he murmured.

Alison pressed her lips together in remembered anger. "You better believe that I'm against it. It'll ruin the town. Fairfax is a nice, quiet place, and I want it to stay that way," she added vehemently.

Matt leaned back against the blue velvet chair and twirled his wineglass by its stem. His well-manicured fingers were lean and strong. Alison noticed that he wore no rings. "But a resort will bring business to Fairfax," he drawled.

"That's what my opponent said," was Alison's rejoinder, her nostrils flaring, "but he lost. Look, Matt, I'm fighting for a certain quality of life in Fairfax. It's not a cut-and-dried question of finances."

"And when does the town vote on zoning take place?"

Something in the tone of his seemingly relaxed drawl made Alison look up at him suspiciously. "Why are you so interested in the doings of Fairfax?" she countered.

17

He was saved from answering by the waiter, who brought them their coffee. By the time Alison had added the sugar and cream to her cup, her mind had veered off the subject of Fairfax onto the closer and more pertinent question of the bill. Now that this pleasant dinner was coming to an end, she knew that she would be facing the moment of truth.

"Matt . . ." she began hesitantly.

"Would you like to have a drink in The Penthouse?" Matt interjected smoothly. "You'll have a wonderful view of Key West." Something flared deep in his eyes as he watched her face, and for a moment Alison had a nagging feeling that maybe it was time to go back to her apartment. But then he smiled boyishly, and she shrugged her doubts aside. One little drink in the bar wouldn't spell disaster, she decided.

"Sure," she said.

They both stood up, and Matt walked around the table to pull out Alison's chair and take her arm. As he came closer to her, Alison looked up in surprise. With her own height of five feet nine inches and the additional three inches of high heels, Alison was accustomed to dwarfing the average man. But Matt stood a powerful six and a half feet or more, she judged, as the top of her blond head came only to his chin. Involuntarily, she shuddered slightly. There was an aura to Matt of unleashed and untamed masculine strength, and not even the conservative cut of his blazer and white slacks disguised the width of his shoulders or the broadness of his chest, which tapered to narrow hips and long, muscular legs.

They were almost out of the restaurant when Alison suddenly realized that they had never been presented with a bill.

"Wait a minute . . ." she cried, and turned to walk back to the table.

Matt stopped and grabbed her arm. "Where are you going?"

"They forgot to give us our bill!"

With a maddening leisure, Matt held on to her arm and glanced over her from the ash-blond hair down to the tips of her white high heels. Alison doubted if he missed an inch. His eyes lingered over the buttons on her bodice, the tight cinch of her belt, the blue silk as it curved over her slender hips, and the slit that ran up one side of her skirt. "Don't worry," he said with amusement; "I'm paying the bill." He guided Alison firmly through the restaurant door.

"Now just a minute," she protested. "I don't let strangers pay for my dinners."

"No?" He kept one hand firmly under her elbow as he pressed the elevator button. His handsome profile looked formidable.

"Of course not," she countered furiously and tried to wrench her arm from his strong grip in a way that wouldn't attract attention.

Alison didn't have a chance against Matt's superior strength. He firmly propelled her into the elevator as its door slid open. "Forget it," he said when they were inside. "The bill is nothing."

"What do you mean, nothing?" Alison countered, helplessly watching the elevator door close. "It's a week's wages. I absolutely insist upon paying you."

Matt shrugged his broad shoulders, as if the subject weren't worth discussing. "Send it to charity."

Alison looked at him in consternation. "Look," she said emphatically, "I want to pay you."

For a moment they both watched the elevator indicator. When it stopped at the sixth floor, Matt said, "It's not necessary. I own this hotel."

"You . . . you own it?" Incredulous, Alison allowed Matt to guide her out into a carpeted corridor and then up a short flight of stairs.

He owned the Hotel Amérique! Alison was dumbfounded and barely noticed when they arrived at a set of carved wooden double doors which Matt had to open with a key. It wasn't until she was ushered into a sunken, dimly lit living room, luxuriously decorated with brown leather couches and thick white carpeting, that Alison came to the realization that she wasn't in the Penthouse Bar at all but in Matt's own apartment.

"Just a minute," she said suspiciously, turning to Matt as he stepped down into the living room. "I thought we were going to The Penthouse."

"This is the penthouse—apartment," he said, emphasizing the pause with a slight smile. Then he pulled open the dark-gold draperies that lined one wall to reveal an immense spread of glass.

For the moment Alison forgot her predicament and, with a delighted exclamation, stepped forward to look at the panoramic view. Spread beneath her was a vista of Key West and the Atlantic Ocean beyond. In the gathering dusk, the lights of the city had begun to sparkle and gleam like a treasure chest of diamonds. Alison could see the landing lights for Key West's small airport and beyond them the winding curve of Roosevelt Boulevard, the beach road that circled the peninsula like a bracelet.

Beyond the land, the ocean stretched as far as the eye could see. The sun had almost set and the water's rippling waves reflected its passing with a rainbow array of colors—from an incandescent yellow to a deep blood-red. The blue sky above had darkened to deep indigo, and the clouds that streaked across it were tinged with orange and pink.

"It's magnificent," she breathed and turned to face Matt.

He had disappeared, and Alison found herself in the living room alone. What was she going to say to him when he returned? Despite the fact that she felt slightly panicked at finding herself alone with him in his apartment, Alison reassured herself that she could handle the situation. After all, she and Matt were adults, and when he came back she'd confess everything and they'd have a good laugh over her case of mistaken identity. And then, after a friendly drink, she'd go back to her hotel.

Satisfied that her problem could be easily solved, Alison wandered around the room, admiring Matt's taste. One wall was lined with books, and she scanned the titles. The authors ranged from classical to modern, and the subject matter was diverse. If Matt's library was an indication of his interests, then he was as well educated as any college professor. The living room's far wall was filled with paintings, original oil colors that were modern but not, Alison noted with relief, overly avant-garde. She sat down on one of the couches and, slipping off her high heels, rubbed her feet in the carpet's thick pile.

"An after-dinner drink, Alison?" Matt walked calmly back into the room and stood near a buffet that held a tray with a cut-glass decanter and glasses. "A cognac, or perhaps a Grand Marnier?"

"A little Grand Marnier with ice, please."

Matt fixed her drink and poured himself a small brandy, then sat on the couch next to Alison. After handing her the small goblet, he stretched one arm across the back of the couch so that it touched her bare shoulders. His dark eyes gleamed at her sardonically.

Alison sat forward as if she'd been touched by an electrical shock. She tried, with a nonchalant air, to slip on her shoes and pull her purse over one shoulder. Then she walked hastily over to the window. "It's a beautiful view," she said, hoping that her nervousness wasn't apparent. She desperately tried to think of the best way to begin telling Matt of the evening's charade.

"I'm glad you enjoy it."

"You know," she began hesitantly, "I thought The Penthouse was the name of a bar."

"Really?" One dark eyebrow arched up in a mocking fashion.

Alison swallowed painfully. She could see that the

21

task she had set herself was not going to be as easy and as simple as she had first conceived. "I really had no idea it was your apartment."

"How interesting," he drawled.

Alison turned and faced the window, but this time she completely ignored the magnificent view before her. The best thing to do, she decided, was just to announce that she was an impostor and get it over with. "Matt . . ."

"Perhaps you'd like a tour of the penthouse?" Matt was standing next to her, although she hadn't even heard him approaching. For a man of his size, he moved like a panther.

"I'd . . ." Alison found the temptation to put off her confession too much to resist. "I'd love that."

"Good. This way, then."

He led Alison first to the dining room, which was as modern and as elegantly decorated as the living room. She suspected that Matt did a great deal of entertaining, for his large teak table could seat twelve. A magnificent wooden breakfront sat against one wall, while the opposite wall was partially concealed by a large Chinese screen. Even from the doorway, Alison could see that its three panels were made of luminous mother-of-pearl and ebony and that the hunting figures on it were as finely wrought as delicate filigree. The living room's white carpet extended into the dining room and enhanced the deep browns of the furniture. A glass and brass chandelier completed the ambiance of modernity and sophistication.

"And the kitchen," Matt announced in a mockingly grandiloquent tone, his arm making a sweeping gesture at the gleaming white and chrome fixtures and at the enormous butcher block island that stood in the center.

"Do you cook?" Alison asked, admiring the ultra-modern appliances.

"I once trained to be a Cordon Bleu chef."

"Oh!" she said, taken aback. It was not quite the answer that she had expected.

Matt grinned at her. "Don't you believe that men can cook? Or aren't you liberated enough for that?"

Alison bridled. "Of course I know that men can cook."

The apartment had two wings off the living-room complex. One wing housed Matt's office, a spare and utilitarian room, plus a conference center which, in addition to a long wooden table and leather chairs, had walls covered with blueprints and maps of the United States.

"Does your business take you all over the country?" Alison asked as her eyes roamed the walls.

"Sometimes." His answer was curt and his tone was cold. Alison surmised that Matt Edwards did not like to discuss his business life.

The other wing housed the bedrooms.

"Oh—how . . . er, nice," Alison murmured, blushing as Matt opened the door to the master bedroom. Although his room was as masculine as Alison would have expected, she was surprised at its austerity. For some reason she had anticipated a playboy's room with a circular bed, perhaps a fur bedspread, and stereo equipment. But the decoration was plain and simple—a large queen-size bed with a navy-blue spread and several dressers.

"And here's a room for you." Back in the hall, Matt's hand rested on the doorknob of what Alison assumed was a second bedroom.

"For me?" Alison wasn't sure that she had heard him correctly.

Matt looked into her shocked blue-green eyes. "For you to freshen up in, if you like." His voice was mocking, and his dark eyes held a strange glint.

"Oh," Alison said in a confused voice.

Matt opened the door and put his hand firmly on the

small of Alison's back and pushed her in gently. "I'll be back in a minute."

Alison stood there indecisively, her drink in her hand, wondering what to do. The room she had entered was a bedroom far more feminine than the master bedroom. The walls were painted a pastel blue and the carpet was a shade of muted green. A small lamp on a night table cast a soft yellow light over the double bed's quilted blue-green spread, on which a sheer white nightgown was tossed as if the room were just waiting for an occupant.

Alison stared at the flimsy nightgown for one bewildered minute before all the puzzling events of the evening clicked firmly into place. When she realized what had happened, she gasped in horrified shock. The wine and the free dinner all pointed to one obvious, glaring conclusion. Matt Edwards thought she was a call girl! Even the fact that he had not known who his date was fit the circumstances.

Alison stood frozen into place. How could she have gotten herself into such a situation? If only she hadn't yearned for a small adventure before her vacation ended. Then she wouldn't have been tempted to go to the Pavillon or to buy a dress that so provocatively outlined all her most obvious assets. Alison blushed to think what she looked like. No wonder Matt Edwards had assumed that she was the right woman.

If only she had nipped the charade in the bud. It would have been so simple to have told Matt that she wasn't his date right at the beginning. Then she wouldn't be in this horrible, embarrassing predicament. He would have left politely; she would have eaten her dinner alone and returned to her hotel safe and sound. Alison groaned slightly. She had no one to blame but herself. The truth was that when Matt Edwards, tall and handsome, had assumed that she was his date, Alison had succumbed to the exciting prospect of being someone else.

The bedroom's second door opened and Matt Edwards appeared. Alison had only one second of logical thought—that this room must be connected to the master bedroom—before she was turned into a frightened, quivering mass of protoplasm by his appearance. Except for a white towel tied casually about his hips, Matt Edwards was completely naked.

He exuded an aura of powerful and awesome masculinity. Alison saw a wide chest, tanned to mahogany, with a diamond of black hair, and a pair of long legs whose muscular thighs gleamed in the lamplight.

"What? You still have your clothes on?"

Shocked, Alison looked into Matt's face. His dark eyes were sardonic and his mouth tilted up into a mocking grin. He looked assured, confident, and virile.

"I . . . I . . ." Alison was struck dumb. Desperately, she kept her eyes on his face.

"Well, I'm ready, even if you're not." With that, Matt placed one hand on the towel at his waist as if to pull it off.

Alison bolted. Still holding on to her glass of Grand Marnier, she turned on her heel and began to run as if her life depended on it. Without looking behind her she dashed down the hall into the living room and yanked at the front door. To her overwhelming relief, it wasn't locked. Leaving it wide open, she ran out into the corridor and glanced around wildly. A red exit sign caught her eye and she raced down the stairwell until she reached the floor below the penthouse.

Alison stopped and turned around, breathless. No one was behind her, and the empty corridor was as silent and as muted as a church. A quick glance told her that no stairway was immediately handy, and she desperately and repeatedly pressed the elevator button. There was no sign of Matt Edwards, and she doubted somehow that he would chase her, considering his current state of dress. She suddenly noticed the glass in her hand and placed it on the floor beside the elevator.

Someone, she hoped, would eventually notice that it was there.

When the elevator arrived Alison entered it quickly, giving a sigh of relief as it descended to the main floor. But it wasn't until she was out on the street in front of the hotel that Alison felt finally safe.

A warm night breeze caressed her face, and she could smell the salty scent of the ocean. The streetlights were on, and around her crowds of tourists and residents, dressed for the evening, were striding by. Alison took a deep breath and began to walk back to her apartment. Her legs were unsteady and her heart was still thudding from her race to get away from Matt Edwards. When she thought about what had happened, she felt confused, frightened, and embarrassed. She just wasn't the sort of girl who ended up in these sorts of situations! And there was one thing that particularly upset her. She was sure, as she had been running down the hallway of the apartment, that she had heard Matt Edwards laughing. Laughing as if it were all an uproarious, hilarious joke.

Chapter Two

"He what?" Karen Birch turned to her friend with a shocked look on her face.

"I told you, he was laughing."

"After acting as if you were a call girl, he started to laugh when you ran away?" Karen was busy at the stove, mixing a beef casserole for dinner.

"It's strange, isn't it?" Alison nibbled on some carrot sticks from a platter of cut vegetables on the kitchen table.

Karen thought for a moment and then, turning from the stove, waved a wooden spoon in Alison's direction.

"You know something, Alison? I think you deserved it."

"Mmmm," Alison mumbled, her mouth full of carrot.

"You should have told him right away who you were."

"I know I should have," Alison admitted.

Karen began to giggle, and Alison looked at her in surprise. "You want to know something else?"

"What?"

"It's sort of funny."

"What's sort of funny?"

"You being mistaken for a lady of the night."

"Well, the humor of it sure didn't strike me at the time."

Karen turned back to the stove. Alison noted that she moved slowly and carefully, but then Karen was eight months pregnant. She also looked hot and tired, and Alison, chiding herself for not noticing her friend's exhaustion, jumped up. "Here, let me make dinner. You sit down and relax."

Karen settled cautiously into one of the kitchen chairs. "Remember all those boys you dated in college?"

"Barely." Alison lifted the cover off a pot of simmering rice and peered inside.

"That's what I mean. You weren't interested in any of them. And even now, there's not a man you go out with who you think is vaguely attractive. That's why your little Key West adventure is so funny."

Alison lifted the wooden spoon to her mouth and cautiously tasted the gravy. "I don't get it."

"It's like a comedy of errors. Here's you—a woman with a reputation for being aloof—and some tall, dark, and handsome stranger comes along and assumes that you're a call girl."

Alison grimaced slightly. "I can see that it does have *some* humorous aspects, and maybe a few years from now I'll even be able to laugh about it."

There was a moment of companionable silence between the two women. "What was he like, anyway?" Karen asked.

"Who?"

"Come on, Alison, don't be evasive."

"Oh, you mean Matt Edwards."

"Of course I mean Matt Edwards."

Alison walked over to the table and carefully investigated a floweret of broccoli that she picked up from the platter. "He was . . . he was . . . interesting," she finally managed.

Karen grinned. "Well, I guess that's a lot coming from you. Frankly, I think he sounds mysterious and gorgeous."

"I don't care how gorgeous he is. I would never get mixed up with a man who hires call girls. It's disgusting!"

"Maybe it was a joke on you?"

"That doesn't make sense, Karen. I'm sure he really did think I was somebody else."

There was a sudden crash and a loud wail from the adjoining living room. Both Alison and Karen rushed to the door to find two-year-old Jeremy sitting on the floor with a pile of fallen blocks around him. Karen went to pick him up and groaned as she started to lean over.

"Here, let me get him." Alison picked up the crying boy. "You're too big to be carrying him around."

Karen wiped a hand across her damp brow and through her short brown hair. "I know, the doctor told me that a pregnant woman of eight months should take it easy and get plenty of rest. He didn't, of course, recommend how I'm supposed to take care of a busy two-year-old at the same time."

"There, there." Alison soothed Jeremy and rocked him back and forth as he cried into her shoulder. She ran a hand over his tousled brown curls and kissed his wet cheek.

Karen smiled at the picture that Alison and Jeremy made together. "You'd be a great mother, Alison, you really would."

Alison grinned at Karen. "Don't you think I should find a husband first?"

"Don't worry. If I could find George, you'll be able to find someone."

"You didn't find him, Karen, you tripped over him."

The two women smiled at each other and began to laugh. Jeremy, who had quieted down, allowed himself to be placed down on the floor with his blocks, and Alison and Karen relaxed on the couch in the living room.

"Remember that day, Alison?"

"How could I forget it?"

Alison and Karen had been best friends through high school and at the nearby college they had both attended. George Birch, whose father owned Fairfax's only radio station, had gone to the same college, but because he was older than the two girls, they knew one another only by sight. One day Karen had gone to the library to meet Alison. When the two of them had emerged and walked down the steps, deep in conversation, neither had noticed the boy before them, who had stopped to tie his shoelaces. Karen had literally tripped over him and tumbled down the stairs, breaking an ankle en route. George had gallantly carried her to the campus medical center, and over bandages and plaster of paris a romance had developed. They had married as soon as Karen graduated.

Since then, neither of them had given up hope of finding marital bliss for Alison. They had introduced her to college friends of George, had eligible men over for dinner, and arranged blind dates. But nothing had ever worked. Alison, who had majored in communications and media, had gone to work for George's father right after graduation. On his retirement and under George's management, she had become second in command at the radio station. She loved her job and her independence, and never yet had she met a man who tempted her to give up either. She was devoted to George and Karen and was godmother to little Jeremy. After her parents' retirement to Arizona, she considered the Birches as her closest family, and they were all she felt she needed.

Karen looked at Alison, who was sitting back on the sofa, her stockinged feet up on the coffee table and her head resting on the back of the couch. Even in blue jeans and black turtleneck sweater, Alison looked like a fashion model, Karen thought a trifle enviously. She had a figure of sleek, trim lines, a classically lovely profile, and her ash-blond hair was striking. Karen thought that she was wasting her time in Fairfax, but when she expressed this opinion to Alison, her friend denied it vehemently.

"I love Fairfax, Karen. This is where I grew up."

"But there's no future for you here. You're doing a great job for George, but think of the opportunities in New York or California. If you sold your parents' house you could go anywhere."

Alison considered for a minute and then shook her head. "This is home, and I'd miss it if I moved away. Besides, now that I've been elected to the town council I've got an important job to do."

"But you'll never meet anyone here, Alison," Karen wailed. "You can count the number of unmarried men in Fairfax on the fingers of one hand."

"There's always David Gallagher," Alison answered mischievously, naming the son of the town pharmacist.

Karen snorted. "David Gallagher has been running after you since grade three, and I haven't noticed that he's gotten any closer recently."

"Well, it doesn't bother *me;* I like being independent."

Karen thought tenderly of George, little Jeremy, and the baby to come. "I think you'd like the idea of marriage, if you ever gave it a chance."

"It isn't marriage that I don't like, Karen, it's men."

"There's nothing wrong with men."

Alison firmly tucked a blond strand behind one ear. "I haven't met one man who has changed my mind about them. They're stubborn, aggressive, and chauvinistic. Look at Matt Edwards, for example. He treated me like a sex object."

"Come on, Alison, I don't think Matt Edwards is a good example. Look at George."

Alison glanced at Karen with a forgiving eye. "George is a sweetheart, and I'm glad you married him. There aren't many men like George around."

"That's because you've got such a closed mind about them. If you wouldn't treat them like antagonists you'd see how sweet they can be."

"Sweet, my eye." At that moment Jeremy toddled over and placed a toy stuffed rabbit in Alison's lap. She picked him up and hugged him. "Now this is what I call sweet, right, Jeremy? You tell your mommy that when it comes to sweet you've got the market all tied up."

Karen threw her hands in the air. "Okay, I give up; but heaven forbid if the right man comes along. You'd trip over him without even noticing."

Alison looked at Karen over the top of Jeremy's head, and there was a strange look in her blue-green eyes. "No, Karen," she said, her voice serious and thoughtful. "If the right man ever comes along, I'll know him in an instant."

"How's everyone?" George called from the vestibule. A door slammed, and then he appeared in the archway of the living room, still dressed in a coat, gloves, and a light dusting of snow. He was a short, pleasant-looking man with curly brown hair and blue eyes.

"We're relaxing for a few minutes before dinner," Karen called back as he disappeared into the other room to hang up his coat.

"I hope it's gourmet," George said as he reappeared, brushing the snow out of his hair. "I'm starved." He leaned over and picked up Jeremy, who cried with delight as his father bounced him up and down. Then George settled into one of the old but comfortable armchairs. George and Karen's decorating style was of the slapdash variety that relied more on durability than elegance. Their friends were accustomed to perching on the furniture or sitting on the floor in the midst of Jeremy's toys. The atmosphere was always relaxed, and after the pressures her day often entailed, Alison was thankful for that.

George looked over Alison with an approving eye,

taking in her lovely tan. "It looks like your week in Key West did you a world of good."

"It was great." Alison smiled. "The apartment was wonderful, and I really appreciated being able to use it."

"Did you meet anyone exciting?" George grinned at her. He liked to play the older-brother role when it came to the topic of Alison and men.

"Well, not exactly," Alison said, blushing.

"Tell him, Alison; go ahead," Karen insisted, "while I get dinner on the table."

Reluctantly, Alison related the story of her last evening in Key West and the strange encounter with Matt Edwards. To her surprise, George's reaction was different from Karen's. Although he also thought it was rather humorous, he saw Matt Edward's actions in another light.

"I think it sounds like he knew very well that you weren't the woman he was supposed to meet."

"But how could he know that?"

"Because of what you told him. A woman who comes from a small town, has a regular job like yours, and has recently won a place on the town council doesn't usually go out with strange men on dates."

"But then why would he treat me that way—taking me up to his apartment and expecting me to . . . to . . . go to bed with him?" She blushed slightly as she said it.

"Because he was enjoying the adventure as much as you were," George countered. "Look, he arrives at the table, finds an attractive woman there who is obviously not the right one, but she doesn't admit it. Now, you have to agree that the situation is intriguing."

"I don't think a real gentleman would have acted that way," Alison said hotly.

"Nobody said he was a real gentleman." George grinned at her. "Here was this lovely woman who was playing a part, and he decided to see how far she would really go. After all, Alison, you weren't completely honest yourself."

Alison looked uncomfortable, and George laughed. "I don't think a real lady would have acted that way," he added in a teasing tone, imitating Alison's voice.

Alison knew when she was outfoxed. "I know, I know. It was all my fault. Heaven only knows, I'll never do it again," she said ruefully.

"Dinner's on," Karen sang out from the dining room.

After they were settled in their places and a protesting Jeremy had been firmly set into his high chair, the conversation veered from Alison's vacation to the radio station.

"It's been a busy week," George said, helping himself to a mound of rice. "You're going to wish that your vacation had lasted a month instead of a week when you see what's on your desk tomorrow."

"Good or bad?" Alison asked.

"Let's see." George pondered for a moment. "There's the payroll, a week's programming to arrange, an interview with the mayor, several intros to write . . ."

Alison groaned. "You're a slave driver."

". . . and a story to write on skiing at Pigeon's Peak."

Alison tasted the casserole. "Mmmm, delicious, Karen," she said and then turned to George. "Why a story on Pigeon's Peak?"

"I don't think we have enough human-interest stuff to flesh out the week."

"Talking about human interest . . ." Karen began and then launched into a bit of gossip about the next-door neighbors.

As George and Karen talked, Alison's mind busily worked over the idea of a human-interest story about skiing. What would be a good angle? Should she investigate it from the perspective of a really good skier or just a novice? Perhaps interviewing one of the men who worked the tow lifts might be fun. After all, he would see just about every skier on the slope during a day's work. Despite George's warning that she would wish she had extended her vacation, Alison felt a stirring of pleasure. She couldn't wait to get back to work. Life was never boring at the radio station.

"Oh, by the way, Alison, I had an interesting phone call today."

Alison turned from her thoughts to George. "From who?"

"The president of the hotel firm that bought the Derrick farm."

Alison looked up sharply. "Oh, really? And what does he want? Some free publicity?" she said acidly.

"Now, now, Alison," George said soothingly, "sheathe your claws." Alison's opinion of the firm that had purchased the Derrick property was well known in the Birch household. "Apparently the man has decided to come up this weekend and see the property personally."

"So why call the radio station? Why not Mayor Bridges? He'd be all too eager to meet with Fairfax's newest property owner." The mayor's enthusiasm for the proposed resort was a constant thorn in Alison's side.

"I don't think he wanted to put political pressure on anyone. He seemed to know that the town council would be voting on the property zoning in the near future."

"Well, isn't that considerate of him," she said icily.

"Now look, Alison. We can't have a man of Martin Drake's stature coming to Fairfax without some kind of welcome, no matter what your personal opinion is."

"Why not have him over for dinner on Saturday night?" Karen asked as she wiped Jeremy's mouth.

George looked at Karen dubiously. "Do you think you can handle it, sweetheart?"

Karen smiled at him. "Don't you think pregnant mothers make good hostesses?" Despite her cheerful bravado, both George and Alison were all too aware that Karen was finding this second pregnancy difficult. There were dark circles under her eyes and her face was lined with fatigue.

Alison thought of the preparations that would be required for a formal dinner with Martin Drake. In addition to the cooking, Karen would have to clean the house and keep an active Jeremy under restraint. The Birches were accustomed to informal gatherings of friends who were used to the hectic atmosphere. Somehow, she doubted if the wealthy owner of a firm listed among the Fortune 500 would be so accommodating.

"I'll do it," she said firmly.

"What?" Both George and Karen looked at her in astonishment.

"I'll give the dinner."

"But, Alison, you don't even like . . ." Karen stopped abruptly.

"I know that my feelings toward Mr. Drake are somewhat less than cordial, but I'll still make a pleasant dinner, and I'll restrain myself, don't worry." She grinned at their worried faces.

Karen looked at Alison doubtfully. "I really don't mind doing it myself."

"Don't be silly, Karen. Remember what the doctor said—rest and relaxation. You'll kill yourself, shopping and cleaning."

George looked at Alison gratefully and then turned to his wife. "Alison's right, honey. You'll exhaust yourself."

"But Alison works all day . . ." Karen began weakly.

"Nonsense," Alison said firmly. "After my vacation, I have enough energy for twenty dinner parties. Now, you're going to stay home with your feet up, and I'll make the meal. You can come over and enjoy the company."

A look of undisguised relief passed over Karen's weary face. "That would be really nice." She sighed. "I hate to admit it, but I do get so tired sometimes."

Alison and George exchanged a look of triumph. "Good," said George. "I'll phone him and issue the invitation."

Alison briskly put her fork down on her plate. "Does anyone know anything about this man Drake?"

"He's a millionaire," Karen answered, trying to spoon some vegetables into Jeremy's mouth.

"An older man, in his fifties," George added. "I saw a picture of him in the paper a couple of years ago when they ran a series of interviews with business tycoons."

Karen tried to coax Jeremy to eat more. "Come on, sweetie, you liked carrots last night."

Alison watched Jeremy's little face set in stubborn refusal. "I think he's changed his mind."

"Whoever said that women are the only fickle creatures," Karen sighed as she put down the spoon, "obviously never met a two-year-old."

"Down! Down!" Jeremy cried, and George got up and pulled the child out of his high chair.

Alison watched Jeremy toddle off toward a box of toy trucks and cars. Her face was thoughtful. "I wonder," she mused, "whether it might be possible to change Mr. Drake's mind about the Derrick property."

George looked at her in surprise. "How?"

Alison started to gather up the dishes. "Maybe if I gave him a real hometown meal and showed him what a nice little town this is, he might be convinced that his resort will only be a detriment to Fairfax, not an asset."

As she was walking into the kitchen with the serving dishes Karen said, "I think you're a dreamer, Alison. That man's spent plenty buying the Derrick farm. He's not going to give up his plans that easily."

"And," George added, "remember what you said in

your campaign—Drake has no real interest in Fairfax's welfare. He's strictly out for himself."

Alison paused. "I know that, but perhaps there's a chance that he can be persuaded to keep his schemes small. The trouble is that right now we just don't have any idea *what* he's planning. For all we know, he might have decided to pave the whole place over and make it a roller-skating rink."

Karen appeared in the kitchen doorway. "Anyone for coffee and cake?"

Over dessert, the conversation turned back to the subject of the proposed dinner party. Since Alison had now agreed to take on the responsibility of entertaining Martin Drake, she decided that she'd give him a real taste of country cooking. "How about a shepherd's pie?" she suggested.

"Too mundane," George objected. "This guy is going to be used to French cuisine."

"Well, he'll have to remember that he's not in France," she said with asperity.

"Why not serve a menu that's based on foods that are grown here," Karen suggested. "Like a beef roast, your mother's potato-squash casserole, and a pie made with the apples from the Lowrys' orchard. I've got a bushel of them in the basement."

"Just spice it up with your sweet and lovely personality, Alison, and it'll be a big hit." George laughed at her.

Alison wrinkled her nose at him. "I promise that I'll be nice to Mr. Drake, but don't think I'm going to let him get off easily. I've got some tough questions for him to answer."

Later that evening, as Alison walked home, her thoughts kept swerving from the problem of Martin Drake to the enigma that was Matt Edwards. The incident in Key West had been far more disturbing than she had let on to Karen and George, and it had shaken her usual composure. Matt's laughter as she ran from the scene of seduction had humiliated her more than she liked to admit. And then there was the haunting memory of his very masculine charms. Alison's feelings, a combination of chagrin, embarrassment, and physical attraction, made the blood rush to her cheeks, and she was thankful for the concealing darkness of night.

To clear her mind of its unpleasant thoughts, Alison looked up at the sky. The night above Fairfax was as black and clear as only nights in the country can be. Without the glare of city lights or an atmosphere smoky from industrial pollutants, the moon and stars gleamed and sparkled as if they had been created anew. The air was clear and cold, and the recent snowfall had coated the trees and the streets with a fresh whiteness. The snow beneath Alison's boots crackled as she walked, and a chilly wind was making the tip of her nose feel like an iceberg. She smiled and ran one gloved hand over a snow-encrusted hedge. Much as she had enjoyed the Florida sunshine, she also loved the crisp, clean bite of winter.

As her cheeks reddened in the wind Alison's thoughts turned to Fairfax. The town lay nestled in a small valley created by low, rolling hills and looked as if nature herself had designed it to fit there. There was a short main street and a cluster of town houses. Beyond lay farms with rich fields that looked like a patchwork quilt when seen from the air. No factory marred the landscape; no mining firm had ever stripped the land bare. The thought of a resort, and the traffic it would bring to Fairfax, made Alison want to grind her teeth in frustration. She knew that many Fairfax businessmen looked forward to a tourist trade, particularly in the winter, when the summer influx of city dwellers in search of lake cottages had gone and only the townspeople remained. Some of the members of the council, members who supported Martin Drake's acquisition of the Derrick property, hoped that the proposed resort would include winter activities like additional ski trails on the surrounding hills, a curling rink, and even a new ice-skating arena.

But Alison couldn't see it from that point of view, and many local residents had supported her contention that towns like Fairfax were a rare and ever-dwindling commodity in the modern, urban world. Fairfax's very smallness was one of its most important assets. Almost everyone knew everyone else. The town had a coziness and friendliness that didn't exist in a big, bustling city. Alison could list the complaints about small towns by heart, the pettiness, nosiness, and claustrophobia, but she also knew that, for her, the warmth of small-town life was precious beyond measure, and she'd fight for it with all her might.

Alison was still deep in thought as she turned up the front path before her house and walked onto the porch. As she dug in her purse for her keys, a frantic scratching behind the door diverted her attention and she began to smile.

"Here I am, Samson. Here I am." She pulled her gloves off and picked up the kitten with a swooping gesture as soon as she stepped inside. The cat, a furry ball of silver and black and white, began to purr immediately, his green eyes, with their large black pupils, gleaming at her, catching the overhead light in their depths.

"Missed me, didn't you?" Alison murmured and pressed her face into his warm fur. Samson purred back in even more passionate enthusiasm.

"Do you mind if I get my coat off, you selfish little beast?" Alison put Samson back down on the hall floor, where he scampered around on tiny legs and meowed at her, his tail sticking up like a tiny exclamation point.

"You don't fool me for a minute," Alison spoke to the kitten who was now winding his way between her legs. "It isn't me you want at all—it's supper you're after." She hung up her coat, switched on the lights, and walked into the kitchen.

Soft yellow lights illuminated the old-fashioned kitchen, which was of the same vintage as the house. Alison's mother had never wanted to replace the old, sturdy cabinets or install the latest appliances. She had grudgingly allowed a small gas range to be placed near the black wood-burning stove but had refused a dishwasher. Her only real concession to modern living had been the refrigerator-freezer which gleamed white in one corner. Not until she and Alison's father had retired to Arizona, into a newly built condominium, had her dislike for "those newfangled contraptions" turned into pleasure.

Alison liked the big old kitchen the way it was and resisted any schemes for remodeling that George and Karen had proposed to her. She was, she reflected as she filled Samson's dish, an old-fashioned sort of person, and not only in terms of modern appliances and conveniences. In her heart, she longed for a return to old-fashioned values and virtues. She had spoken a half-truth to Karen. She really didn't dislike men in general—only modern men. As far as she was concerned, modern men had only one purpose in taking out a woman—and that was to get her into bed with them. Alison had been subjected to enough unwanted passes and embarrassing tussles to last her a lifetime. She knew that she was beautiful, and she often cursed that beauty. Because of it, the men she had dated had seen her more as a trophy for display than as a friend who had the potential of developing a serious and loving relationship.

Alison placed Samson's dish down on the linoleum floor with such vehemence that the little kitten jumped away in alarm. While she knew that she was to blame for what had happened at the Hotel Amérique, the incident had only reinforced her opinion of today's men. Matt Edwards was the very epitome of the type of man she despised. All his charm and attractive masculinity could not blind Alison to the fact that Matt had had one purpose in mind: an emotionless and loveless sexual encounter.

Alison stalked into her bedroom and flipped on the lights, revealing a large four-poster bed with a handmade quilt in reds and blues. The sight of its geometric pattern soothed her nerves. The quilt had been a part of her life since she was a baby. Her grandmother had made it for Alison's hope chest, starting it a week after Alison had been born and finishing it just before her death a year later. Alison thought that there were few men in this world who would appreciate the family traditions behind that carefully handsewn quilt. And certainly not Matt Edwards, who saw a woman only in terms of her body, without seeking the personality and the soul that lay within.

Alison tugged off her turtleneck shirt and jeans and lifted a warm blue flannel nightgown out of her dresser drawer. Just before she pulled it over her head she caught sight of her reflection in the long mirror on her closet door. Her body was long and slender, with firm breasts and gently curving hips. She blushed when she thought of the way Matt Edwards had run a practiced eye over her dress as if he could see the skin that lay beneath it. Until her dying day she knew she would regret that small desire for adventure that had led her into such a difficult situation. Only the knowledge that she would never lay eyes on Matt Edwards again had saved her from hours of excruciating embarrassment.

Alison wrapped herself in a long, fluffy yellow robe and tied its cord firmly around her waist. She picked up Samson, who had come wandering into the bedroom and was carefully investigating the contents of the handbag she had thrown on the floor at her feet.

"How about some television and then bedtime, little pussycat?" she whispered into his tiny velvety ear.

42

Samson flicked his ear and licked her hand. "I knew you'd agree," Alison commented to the kitten as she carried him into the living room and settled down into the big, old-fashioned armchair. "You're the only male I know who is completely agreeable and totally uncomplicated."

Despite the kitten's warm purring and the canned laughter coming from the television, Alison found that one emotion continued to upset and perplex her. It was an emotion that she had tried to forget and to suppress. Yet no matter how hard she denied it to herself or concealed it from an astute friend like Karen, it refused to be hidden or forgotten. When Matt Edwards had walked into that bedroom, nude except for a brief, clinging towel, a hot flame had shot through her, making her head swim and her legs go weak. No man had ever caused her to feel that way before, and she hoped that no man ever would again. It came from a fire within herself that Alison had not known existed, one that she was determined to quench. It threatened her stability and her peace of mind; it threatened the very image that she carried of herself. Alison was reluctant to put a name to it, but she knew all too well what it was. The flame of desire had licked at her cool and aloof heart, and she had trembled before its force.

Chapter Three

Alison carefully opened the oven door and tried to peer in at the apple pie which sat on the top rack, but the moist, damp heat made her pull away sharply. The pie should be done, she speculated and, pulling on a pair of oven mitts, took it out of the oven. The top crust was crisp and golden and a delicious odor of hot apple and cinnamon steamed out of the diagonal cuts. Alison gingerly put a sharp knife into the pie and then sighed gratefully. Done, and right on time, too.

She took the squash casserole from the counter and placed it on the lower rack next to the cut of beef that was already roasting and closed the door. Brushing her hands on her apron, Alison walked into the living room to check that all her preparations were finished. The house could pass a military inspection, she decided as she stared at her reflection in the gleaming mahogany top of the coffee table. A fire crackled in the large stone fireplace and Samson lay curled in the big green armchair with curving arms that stood to one side of it. The lamps on the end tables shone on the high-backed green sofa and threw warm yellow beams onto the oval green-and-white hooked rug that lay on the dark wooden floor.

Alison looked it all over with an appreciative eye. It might not be decorated in a style sophisticated enough for a millionaire like Martin Drake, but it was perfect for Alison Ramsey. She walked over to the front door and switched on the porch light. Pulling aside the white gauze curtain which covered the windowpane in the door, she gazed out into the dusk. Alison shook her head in doubt and concern. Snow had been falling since morning, and now the wind was beginning to rise. Large flakes of snow were blowing down the street in great white bursts. Occasionally, the whirling flakes were so thick that they even blurred the light from the streetlamp in front of the house. As she stood watching, a car with chains on its tires drove slowly down the street, its windshield wipers moving steadily to remove the quick accumulation of snow.

Alison walked back into the kitchen, wondering whether she had cooked dinner in vain. Although there had been no word from Martin Drake, who, she presumed, was now driving to Fairfax, there seemed to be a good chance that he wouldn't be able to make it, considering the weather. This morning's predicted light snowfall had developed into this afternoon's storm and was fast turning into tonight's blizzard. With a vague feeling of worry, Alison hoped that he wasn't caught in a snowdrift somewhere along the highway.

Alison took off her apron and walked upstairs to her bedroom. It was still too early to expect her guests, which gave her time to check her makeup and clothes. Although she wanted to give Martin Drake a taste of Fairfax's unique small-town flavor with a homey meal and a cozy atmosphere, Alison didn't want him to think that Fairfax's residents were country bumpkins. She had dressed with special care, choosing a navy-blue, long-sleeved wool dress with cuffs and collar in white lace. The dark blue heightened the blue in her eyes, which she emphasized with a touch of mascara and eye shadow. Glancing in her full-length mirror, Alison mentally nodded in approval. With her high heels and the simple, elegant line of her dress she looked feminine, and yet precise, as well. Just the right touch for an evening that promised to be a mixture of business and pleasure.

Alison was giving one last brushing to her sleek blond hair when the doorbell rang. A quick glimpse out her bedroom window showed a long, gleaming gray Ferrari with skis on the roof. As she walked down the stairs Alison frowned in confusion. It was too early for Martin Drake, and she could not think of any acquaintance who owned a Ferrari. Perhaps some stranger who had lost his way was stopping for directions.

Without glancing through the window first, Alison pulled the door open and then gasped. There was no mistaking the tall man who stood on her porch. Despite the snow that sat like a cap on his dark hair and clung to his shoulders like a lacy shawl, Alison would have known that face anywhere.

"Evening, Alison," Matt Edwards said, his strong white teeth gleaming in a wicked grin. When she didn't answer, he looked at her quizzically. "Aren't you going to say hello?" The look in his dark eyes was amused, mocking, and smug.

Regaining her senses, Alison moved quickly and tried to shut the door with a furious, definitive slam. There was a loud screech at her feet, and she looked down with horror to see that she had caught Samson's tail between the door and the doorjamb.

"Blast!" she hissed under her breath and pulled the door open again. To her relief, Samson ran off without further ado. She looked up to find Matt Edwards still standing there, his smile even wider. Alison narrowed her eyes at him and made ready to slam the door once again when the phone began to ring insistently. Shaken, her heart pounding in heavy thumps, she stood indecisively for a moment and then ran into the kitchen to answer the phone.

It was George. "Alison, it's me." His voice was breathless in her ear. "Karen has gone into labor and I'm taking her to the hospital."

The news about Karen made Alison forget the man who stood at her front door. "Oh, George, is she okay? Isn't it too early?"

"Only a couple of weeks," George replied. "Everything seems to be fine. Her mother is here to stay with Jeremy."

"You'll let me know the minute . . ."

"Of course," George answered. "Listen, I'm sorry about the dinner tonight. You're going to have to entertain Martin Drake yourself."

"It's okay, George," she answered with more steadiness than she truly felt. "I'll manage. Just give my love to Karen."

"Right." George hung up but Alison stood there, rooted to the ground, holding the silent phone in her hand. When she looked up, Matt Edwards was standing beside her.

"Finished?" he asked in a mocking voice.

When she didn't answer, he gently took the phone from her hand and placed it back in its cradle. With a deep breath Alison turned slowly to face him. The snow in his hair was melting and the ends curled slightly around his forehead and ears. He had taken off his coat and in his arms, against his broad sweater-covered chest, he cradled a purring Samson. The kitten looked tiny and vulnerable in his large, strong hands.

"Finished," she said, clearing her throat with a slight cough.

"Not sick, are you?" His voice held not the slightest tinge of sympathy.

"Of course not," she replied and then steeled herself. It was time to let Matt Edwards know, in no uncertain terms, that she wanted him out of her house, and pronto. "Will you—" she began.

He didn't let her finish. "Don't you owe me something?" He looked her over in a predatory way and Alison found herself shivering slightly.

47

"Owe you something?" she asked incredulously. "I don't owe you a thing."

"I think you do." His lips curled up in amusement and there were deep and mocking glints in his eyes. With a calm motion, he lowered Samson to the floor. There was a short silence as the kitten sniffed at the heel of his brown leather boot and then scampered away.

"I want you out of my house," Alison said through clenched teeth.

"Not until I receive some payment," he responded, advancing toward her. He was huge and menacing, with an unmistakable gleam in his dark eyes. Alison illogically found herself thinking that no man had a right to such dark, thick, and curling eyelashes. Then she shook herself and dropped her eyes from his face to the sweater that covered his muscular chest. It was dark blue, and Nordic in style, with an intricate red-and-yellow pattern knitted into its yoke. It made his already broad shoulders seem even broader. It also made a permanent imprint on Alison's brain. It came closer and closer and Alison knew she'd never forget that design as long as she lived.

She found her voice. "Payment for what?" she finally said, running her tongue over dry lips as she backed slowly into the hall.

"For a nice evening," he replied, his eyes intent on her tongue and mouth.

"I sent it to charity, as you suggested," Alison said desperately.

"I've changed my mind," he said smoothly. "'Charity begins at home.'" And then, as easily as if Alison were tiny and helpless like Samson, Matt gathered her into his arms and pressed his lips down to hers.

At first Alison resisted him and tried to push his body away from hers, only to discover that his chest was hard and unyielding. Her frantic motions only served to

48

make him pull her even closer until her breasts were crushed against him and she could feel the pressure of his muscular thighs against hers. Matt Edwards was taking his sweet time kissing her. At first his warm lips played with hers and his tongue moved softly until he found her teeth. Alison clamped her jaws shut and began to yank at his thick hair with determined hands.

He lifted his head for a moment and looked down into her widened aquamarine eyes. "For a woman who likes to go out with strangers, you're awfully resistant," he drawled and with one hand lazily caught her two hands and held them behind her back.

"It was a mis—" Alison started to speak, but his mouth cut her off. He gave her no time to close her mouth, and his tongue invaded while his hard lips pressed hers open. Sensations that Alison had been trying to stave off for a week now came rushing back. Her head began to swim as a seductive warmth stole over her. Matt, sensing that she no longer wished to hold him off, became gentler, and his mouth moved over hers in a sensual, probing way. Not until he took his mouth from hers and began to explore her jawline and the tip of her ear with his lips did Alison come to her senses.

She pushed him away, and this time Matt let go of her and stepped back. He looked her over with the same audacity that she recalled from that evening in Key West. With a slow and languorous glance he took in the disheveled strands of her hair, the luminous gaze of her blue eyes, and her slightly parted pink lips. He grinned at her.

Alison stiffened and wordlessly pushed past him, marching into the living room and up to the front door. She threw it open and pointed into the snowstorm. "Out!" she said.

"My, my," Matt scolded, "aren't we just a bit . . . impolite?" He walked over to the big armchair, picked up Samson, who was curled up there, and sat down comfortably with the kitten on his knee.

"I mean it." This time she spat out the words. "Get out!"

Matt Edwards leaned back in relaxation and began to stroke Samson, running his long fingers over the kitten's black-striped fur. "You're causing quite a draft, leaving the door open," he said pointedly.

Alison gritted her teeth and slammed the door in fury. She marched back into the living room and sat in the rocking chair opposite Matt.

"Now, look," she said in a falsely conversational way, "you can't stay here."

"No?"

"No," she said emphatically.

"Any particular reason that I can't warm myself by your crackling fire while winter rages outside?"

"Don't get poetic with me," Alison retorted furiously.

"Why, Alison Ramsey," he said in a wondering voice, "I do believe you're just the slightest bit annoyed with me."

"Matt, I want you out of here. This instant."

Matt lifted Samson until the kitten's tiny triangular face was level with his own laughing dark eyes. "You know something, friend? I think she'd throw me out into that blizzard if she could. Now, is that the way for a good hostess to act?"

"I am *not* your hostess," Alison said, raging at him.

Matt lifted his chin and sniffed. "That's funny," he said. "I could have sworn that I smelled dinner cooking. Not to mention the lovely table." He waved his arm at the open dining-room door. Inside, Alison had laid out her mother's best linen tablecloth, the white bone china with the blue willow pattern, and her own sterling silver.

"That's not for you. It's for someone else."

"And who is the lucky man?"

"None of your business. Now, get out." She leaned forward to emphasize her point.

"There she goes again." Matt once more addressed Samson, and the tiny kitten placed one soft paw trustingly on his hard shoulder.

Alison decided to try another tack. "Matt, that evening in Key West was a big mistake."

Matt heaved a huge sigh. "Now she tells me." He placed Samson on his broad shoulder, where the kitten curled up next to his ear and started to purr.

"It's my fault, and I should have explained the whole thing to you right away," Alison went on, "but . . . but . . ."

"I'm listening," Matt said airily.

"I had made a reservation for myself alone, but when I got there the maître d' assumed I was someone else and sat me at your table."

Matt arched one eyebrow at her. "And you've always wanted to be an actress, so when I arrived you just impersonated my dining companion."

Alison sighed. "It's not that I wanted to be an actress. It's just that . . . well, at the moment it seemed like fun, and I . . ." Her voice trailed off awkwardly.

Matt scrutinized her pink cheeks and grinned. "Well, you didn't do too badly," he said with false sympathy.

"That's not the point," Alison cried. "The point is that I had no intention of going to b . . . to your apartment with you."

"Really?" he drawled.

"And then when I saw that nightgown, I . . . I . . ." Alison couldn't finish her sentence.

"You chickened out, as they say in the vernacular," Matt finished it for her with a mocking smile on his handsome face.

"No!" Alison cried furiously. "I didn't 'chicken out.' Believe me, I never intended to . . . anything more than the dinner."

Matt looked her over with a lazy, roaming eye,

51

taking in her lovely blushing face, the tilting blue-green eyes with their dark lashes, and her smooth curtain of white-blond hair. "Too bad," he murmured.

Alison felt herself turning a deeper pink, and she quickly looked down at her toes. "Please," she whispered to the floorboards, "please, go away."

"Into the blizzard?" Matt said in a seemingly incredulous voice.

"There's a hotel in Fairfax. It's about half a mile away," she said desperately.

"You'd send me out into a blizzard without dinner?"

Alison looked back into Matt's eyes, where warm lights danced at her through his dark lashes. "Matt, please," she begged, "I told you that I have another guest."

"Who?"

"Will you go if I tell you?"

"Cross my heart." He grinned at her, and Alison was forcibly reminded of his undeniable charm.

"A businessman named Martin Drake. He's driving up from a hotel in the Poconos."

"No problem," Matt said jauntily.

Alison looked at him wearily. "It *is* a problem. You can't stay here when Martin Drake comes."

"Of course I can."

Alison began to grow angry again and, standing up, she pointed her finger imperiously to the front door. "You can't. Now, get out, please—you said you'd go if I told you his name."

Matt kept a completely straight face. "But, Alison," he said, "I *am* Martin Drake, but please call me Matt—everyone else does."

Alison swallowed painfully and bit her lower lip. Then, slowly but gradually, she sat back in the rocking chair. For a few seconds she closed her eyes as if she could erase Matt Edwards from her sight and rocked gently back and forth as if the motions could ease her agitation. Finally, she opened her eyes and looked at the man who sat so nonchalantly opposite her. He was, she noted, handsomer than she remembered, and twice as infuriating. "Say that again, please," she asked in a low voice.

"Martin Matthew Edwards Drake, Miss Ramsey, at your service." He stretched his long legs toward the fire. The jeans he wore were molded to his muscles like a second skin. "Nice and toasty," he said to no one in particular. Samson uncurled and readjusted his position on Matt's shoulder. As he tucked his tail up to his nose he purred even louder.

You traitor, Alison thought, glaring at the contented kitten. She turned her attention to Matt, who looked for all the world as if he belonged in her armchair. "You lied to me," she said in an accusing voice.

"Not exactly."

"You are a phony, lousy liar." This time she hissed the words at him.

With an amused arch to his eyebrows, Matt took in the sparks in her blue eyes and the high color in her cheeks. His gaze dropped down to the front of her dress just below the delicate lacy collar. In her anger Alison had been breathing furiously and her breasts were rising and falling in a matching tempo. She crossed her arms and Matt grinned at her. "I guess we're just two of a kind." He shrugged his broad shoulders and Samson tumbled down his chest and onto his lap. He grabbed the kitten, who playfully tried to bite Matt's large thumb with his tiny teeth.

"But I told you the truth about myself," she protested.

"Except for the most important part—that you weren't my date."

Alison sighed in resignation. There was no denying her own duplicity in the incident and she was reminded of an old adage that people in glass houses shouldn't throw stones. It was amazing how old adages seemed to apply so well to particularly modern dilemmas, she thought wryly.

Suddenly a thought struck her, and she looked at him with a frown. "But George said that Martin Drake was a man in his fifties."

"My father—he retired about three years ago."

"Oh," Alison said in a muted voice, and then all the ramifications of Matt's confession hit home. "Do you . . . do you mean to say that *you* are the Martin Drake who bought the Derrick property?"

"None other."

"Why, you low-down, miserable sneak!" Alison was thoroughly outraged. "You sat through that entire dinner, knowing exactly who I was and what I was talking about, and you never said a thing!"

Matt looked into Alison's face. Her blue eyes held sparks of angry fire. "Well, I do admit that I was . . . ahem, somewhat surprised," he said, mildly apologetic.

Alison ignored his mild tone. "And . . . and you even found out that there was going to be a vote on the zoning of the property!"

"Now, now, remember, I didn't ask. You volunteered the information."

Alison swept aside his comment with a furious wave of her hand. "So that's why you're here—to influence the town council to vote your way."

Matt calmly stood up and, taking the poker, knelt before the fire and moved one of the burning logs. "It's always good business practice to know the opposition's strategy."

Alison was virtually speechless with rage and glared down at him. "I don't believe it," she whispered to herself.

"There," Matt said, standing up and brushing his hands on his jeans. "I think the fire just needed some encouragement." As if in enthusiastic response, the warm orange flames flared up into the chimney, throwing a reddish glow onto Matt's tanned, clean-shaven cheeks. "Now, how about some dinner? I think I smell something burning."

"Oh, no!" Alison leaped out of the rocking chair and ran into the kitchen. She threw open the oven door and a billow of smoke rolled out into the room. The smell of burning squash filled the air. "Oh, no!" she cried again, pulling out the casserole and staring at it helplessly. It was burned beyond redemption.

"That's too bad." Matt was standing right beside her.

His voice was gentle, and Alison threw him a suspicious look. She had no reason in the world to think that Matt could be even the slightest bit sympathetic. After all, he had entered her house as if he owned it, forced himself upon her with a kiss that demonstrated that he considered her nothing but a sex object, and then had had the audacity to admit that he had lied through his teeth to her. He had, she decided bitterly, no more kindness than a viper.

Alison placed the casserole on the stove top, pulled out the roast, and examined its surface. "I don't think it's burned," she said dubiously, "just overcooked."

"It looks fine," Matt said. "Here, let me help you." He took the pan from Alison's hands and carried it over to the big wooden table that stood in the middle of the kitchen. "I'll carve, if you'll give me a knife."

Alison pulled out the carving board and a knife and handed them to him. She took one last regretful look at the squash casserole and then, opening the refrigerator door, began to investigate the contents of the vegetable bin.

As if they had called a truce, Alison and Matt kept their dinner-table conversation to safe and noncontroversial topics. As Alison had discovered during their evening in Key West, Matt could charm the birds out of the trees. In spite of herself, she found that she enjoyed his company more than she liked to admit. He had a devastating combination of looks, wit, and virility. She would bet her bottom dollar that he had more women falling over him than any one man could handle.

As he finished his coffee, Matt looked at Alison over the brim of his cup. "Not bad for a 'well-done' meal," he quipped.

"You don't have to rub it in," Alison said ruefully. "I know it didn't come up to Cordon Bleu standards."

"The pie was outstanding," Matt conceded.

"The apples came from a local orchard," Alison answered and then threw him a challenging glance. "Just like the one on the Derrick farm."

"Absolutely delicious," he reiterated.

Alison decided to come to the point. "Matt, how committed are you to building a resort?"

"We spent a lot of money investigating this area and buying the property."

"What exactly do you have in mind?"

Matt set his cup carefully back in its saucer and folded his arms. "Something like Manorville," he answered, naming a year-round resort two hundred miles east of Fairfax which housed a large central chalet, a swimming pool, tennis courts, winter and summer trails, and a curling rink.

Alison blanched when she thought of the traffic that would bring to Fairfax. "Have you considered the effect it would have on the area?"

Matt smiled at her. "It will be elegant and tasteful. It won't shame the town."

"That's not the point," Alison cried. "It might not shame Fairfax, but it *will* change it."

"Is change so bad, Alison?" he asked gently.

"*I* think so," she retorted angrily and then forced herself to calm down. The only way to handle a man of Matt's caliber was to remain cool, logical, and rational.

"Not everyone in Fairfax is opposed to a resort," he pointed out.

"How do you know?" she asked suspiciously.

"I had a talk with the mayor a few days ago," he said flatly.

Alison completely forgot her determination to remain calm. She glared at him. "You are an underhanded, sneaking, vicious . . ."

Matt held up a protesting hand. "There's nothing illegal in calling up the mayor."

"You used the information I gave you for your own purposes," she sputtered.

"You gave it free of charge," he said nonchalantly.

Alison was trying to think of a stinging reply when the telephone rang. "Excuse me," she said curtly to Matt and stalked into the kitchen.

"Alison? It's George."

"George!" For a moment Alison felt a twinge of guilt. She had completely forgotten that George had taken Karen to the hospital. "How's Karen?"

"She's fine, and the doctor says everything is progressing normally, but she's still got a few hours to go before the baby will be born."

"You'll call me as soon as anything happens?"

"Don't worry, you'll be the first to know," George replied. "How are you coping? Did Martin Drake show up?"

"He's here right now."

"Everything all right? Can you handle him?" George's voice had a worried tone.

"With both hands behind my back," Alison answered with an irony that was lost on George, but not on Matt. He threw her a quizzical look as he walked into the kitchen bearing a pile of dirty dishes.

"How is your friend?" Matt asked as Alison replaced the phone in its cradle. She had explained the Birches' absence during dinner.

"Karen's doing well, but there's no news yet," Alison responded and followed him into the dining room, where he was efficiently clearing the table.

When he had picked up the last of the dishes, Alison carefully rolled up the linen tablecloth and carried it into the kitchen. She found Matt with his large frame wrapped in an apron, his sleeves rolled up, and his hands in a sinkful of soapsuds.

"You don't have to do that," she protested.

"You'd rather I sang for my room and board?" He lifted a soapy plate from the water and ran a sponge over its surface.

It took Alison a moment to digest the full import of his statement. "What do you mean, 'room and board'?" she asked slowly, taking a dry towel from a drawer and drying the dishes that he had already stacked in the rack.

"Haven't you looked out the window recently?"

"You mean the snow?"

"I mean the blizzard." He emphasized the last word.

Alison switched on the back-door light and peered out into the night. She had completely forgotten about the weather. Outside, she discovered, the snow was flying and the wind gusting with ferocity, the flakes coming down so thickly that she couldn't even see the outline of her neighbor's house. She turned to the kitchen counter and switched on the radio.

". . . winds gusting to forty miles an hour and a predicted snowfall of twenty-two inches by morning," the announcer was saying. "While all major highways are still passable, the police report that they are dangerous and slippery. Many access roads have been closed to cars. Storm warnings have been posted all over upstate New York, and police caution drivers to remain at home except in cases of dire emergency. For further weather bulletins . . ."

Alison turned off the radio, feeling a flutter of panic rising in her chest. Surely this didn't mean that Matt was going to be staying overnight in her house? The strain of the evening had been bad enough. Alison resolved that Matt simply had to leave.

She picked up a wet wineglass and surreptitiously glanced at Matt, who was washing the dishes with an admirable efficiency. His profile was strong and handsome and revealed absolutely no emotion. "You don't . . . you don't think you're staying here for the night, do you?" she asked.

"Do you have any other suggestions?" He calmly rinsed out the roasting pan and set it on the rack, taking a step closer to Alison to do so.

Alison felt her knees go weak as Matt's muscular arm brushed her shoulder. Her flutter of panic was quickly developing into a maelstrom of fear. "You can't stay here!" she said desperately. "It's . . . it's not right!"

Matt took in her widened blue eyes and the look of shock on her face. His lips curled in amusement. "Afraid of what the neighbors might say?"

Alison stiffened. "Gossip doesn't bother me," she replied haughtily, hoping to hide her panic. In truth, she cared very little about what the neighbors would say, but she cared a great deal about her own reactions to Matt's disturbing presence. For the past hour she had tried to forget the kiss he had forced on her and her own aroused emotions. The way she had felt was contrary to every standard that she had ever set for herself. Instead of being aloof, she had become involved; instead of remaining passive, she had been passionate. The thought of another twelve hours of Matt, even asleep in another bedroom, undermined her composure. She had to get him out of the house.

With a determined motion, Alison folded the towel and set it on the counter. She walked quickly out of the kitchen into the hallway and pulled open the closet door. She was pulling out her winter jacket and a pair of high boots when Matt came up beside her.

"What are you doing?"

"I'm digging you out," she said through clenched teeth.

"All by yourself?" He leaned against the doorframe

and watched as Alison groped frantically through a box for her hat.

"If I have to dig all night—the answer is yes." She tugged a blue woolen hat over her hair.

Matt walked over to her and removed the hat strings from her hands. Gently, he tied them under her chin, holding her eyes with his dark gaze. "Does my presence upset you so?"

Alison felt as if she were drowning in the softness of those brown eyes. She quickly pulled away from him and grabbed her boots. "You can't stay here," she answered evasively, avoiding his look.

She zipped up her coat and pulled on her thick woolen mittens. Throwing one last furious look at Matt's amused expression, she walked out the front door and slammed it behind her.

Alison took a deep breath of the cold night air. She had felt as if she were suffocating in the house. Matt's outspoken virility was unnerving, and his innuendo seemed to have set the atmosphere between them afire. Alison grabbed one of the snow shovels that sat against the porch railing and began to dig her way down the porch steps. Ahead of her lay the Ferrari, blanketed by snow, its wheels completely buried in the drifts.

The door opened and closed behind her, and Alison looked up to see an overcoated Matt grab the other shovel. Wordlessly, he stepped before her and began to shovel his way down the steps and onto the pathway. The wind swirled and whistled around them as if it were alive. Alison could feel the flakes being driven into her cheeks like stinging needles. As she worked her way down onto the walk, she cursed her impatience to get outside. She should have changed into slacks. With every step into the drifts she sank almost to her knees and snow slipped down into her boots. She could feel the wind's icy blasts across the back of her legs as the gusts lifted the hem of her dress.

Matt was in front of her, easily lifting and throwing

the heavy shovelfuls of snow off the walk. In his bulky coat, he looked like a giant, his feet planted firmly apart and his shoulders steady against the wind. Gusts whipped at his dark hair, blowing off the snow that had landed on it. His aggressive masculinity, which had so unsettled her in the house, was strangely reassuring now that they were out in the storm. He was an unexpected source of strength and reliability in the midst of the roaring elements.

As Alison watched, Matt made his way to the Ferrari and began to dig out around the door. Alison breathed a small sigh of relief. He did intend to leave after all. She followed him down the narrowly shoveled path and planted her shovel in the snow by the Ferrari's right rear wheel. To her surprise, Matt grabbed her arms.

"Forget it," he yelled over the wind and, letting go of her arm, opened the car door.

"What are you doing?" she yelled back.

"Getting my suitcase."

"But we're digging you out!" she protested, staring into his reddened face. Snow had gathered on his dark lashes and thick eyebrows. He looked menacing and formidable.

"Are you planning to dig out the whole street as well?"

Alison looked beyond the Ferrari to the road. It was covered with snowdrifts that constantly changed shape as the wind blew down the street in heavy blasts. Her heart sank. There was no possible way that Matt could drive down the street. It would be impassable until the blizzard stopped and the snowplows cleared a way. Her shoulders drooped, and Matt patted her on the arm.

"It won't be so bad," he yelled at her and grinned.

Alison turned away and trudged up the pathway. She felt cold, wretched, and discouraged. The snow had melted and was dripping down the inside of her boots, her toes were frozen, and her nose felt like an icicle. The impossible and the unthinkable were happening to her. The most arrogant, infuriating, and irritating man that she had ever had the misfortune to meet was going to be spending the night in her house. Alison had a ball of fear in her stomach that felt icier than the wind. She was fearful of more verbal sparring with Matt and of his unpredictable actions. She was fearful of his physical presence and his forceful masculinity. But most of all, she was fearful of herself. The Alison she knew, the composed and unflappable Alison who could handle any situation with aplomb, had disappeared. In her place another, different Alison had appeared, one who was caught in a whirlwind of emotions. For one moment she had been firm and resistant in the face of Matt's undeniably sexual advances, but in the next moment she had surrendered without warning, drowning in the rushing, swirling tides of her own desires.

Alison trudged wearily into the house and stood there, letting her coat and boots drip onto the hall mat. She had the sinking, frightening feeling that handling Martin Matthew Edwards Drake was going to be the greatest challenge she had ever faced.

Chapter Four

Thick, soft fur waved in front of her face and tickled her nose. Alison tried to turn her head and push the fur away, but her motions were slow and heavy and she could barely lift her arm from her side. The fur pressed closer and closer, and Alison knew with a desperate certainty that she was about to sneeze.

"Ah-choo!" The violent sneeze woke her up and Alison turned to find Samson beside her as she lay tangled in the blankets and sheets. He had placed three black-and-white paws on her pillow and was patting her cheek enthusiastically with the fourth.

"Phooey," she said, wrinkling her nose into his tiny, inquisitive face. "Who invited you?"

She sneezed once more and reached for the box of tissues beside her bed. Her hand stopped in midair when the faint metallic sound of pots and pans banging against one another came through her bedroom door.

Memory flooded through her and Alison sat up straight in bed. For a moment she had completely forgotten that Matt Drake had spent the night in her house, down the hall in the guest bedroom. But, she remembered with an odd irritation, all her fears had come to nothing. His behavior the evening before, when they had returned after the unsuccessful attempt to dig his car out, had been impeccable. He had maintained a gentlemanly distance, avoiding topics with any sexual overtones, and if she hadn't remembered it all too vividly, Alison would have sworn that a different man had forcibly kissed her only hours earlier.

Alison sneezed again, pulled a tissue from the box, and held it against her nose. "Ugh," she said to Samson, who had curled comfortably in her lap. "I think I've got a cold."

She had almost immediately regretted her hasty decision to dig Matt's Ferrari out of the snow without changing into the proper clothing. By the time she had gotten out of her sopping wet clothes into slacks and a sweater she had already developed a small case of the sniffles. Now it seemed that her sniffles had grown into sneezes, which no doubt would develop into a full-fledged cold.

Matt couldn't have been kinder, either. When she had returned to the living room she discovered that he had already made a thorough investigation of her meager liquor cabinet and had mixed her a hot buttered rum. Like some solicitous nanny, he had made sure that she drank it down and then plied her with aspirin, all the while amusing her with light-hearted chatter.

His one and only pass of the evening had occurred when the fire had gotten low and he had suggested that when she went to bed he could tuck her in. Alison had bristled, and Matt had instantly agreed that she was old enough to put herself to bed. The fact that an undercurrent of laughter lay beneath his solemn tone hadn't fooled her in the least. Alison didn't trust Matt. He had lied about who he was, maneuvered politically behind her back, kissed her without provocation, *and* managed to spend the night at her house. She wouldn't have put it past him, she decided wryly, to have created that blizzard all for his own benefit.

Alison blew her nose and got out of bed, gingerly placing her bare feet on the cold wooden floor and shivering in her flannel nightgown. She walked over to the window, pulled aside the heavy curtain, and groaned. It was still snowing outside, although not so heavily and without the gusting, blowing winds. There were high white drifts all around the house and an utter silence—the sort of peacefulness that blankets a town when every house is snowed in. From the looks of the snow-covered street, it was obvious that there was no possible way that Matt could leave right away. Alison knew that the road crews would not begin working until the snowfall stopped or at the very least became considerably lighter. What she was to do with an unpredictable Matt Drake for an entire day she had absolutely no idea.

An increasing clangor from the kitchen drew her attention away from the scene outside her window. She knew from the sounds that Matt must be making breakfast, and from Samson's contented purring on her pillow that he had already been fed. Alison didn't like to admit it, but she had a certain amount of respect for a man who could make himself so painlessly at home as Matt had done in her house.

She pulled on a pair of jeans, a dark blue turtleneck, and a pair of warm, fur-lined moccasins. She glanced at her face in the bathroom mirror and winced. The oncoming cold had made her eyes reddish and tinged her nose an unflattering shade of pink. She combed her blond hair into its usual smooth bell shape and applied some makeup in a vain attempt to camouflage the effects of her cold. With reluctance and a growing feeling of vulnerability, Alison descended the staircase and walked into the kitchen.

In spite of the stuffiness from her cold, the aromas rising from the various pots and pans bubbling and sizzling on the stove were enticing. Matt, whose lean form was wrapped in a voluminous blue-checked apron, had rolled the sleeves of his denim shirt up beyond his elbows and was opening a carton of eggs as she came in.

"Good morning," she said, her voice faintly nasal.

Matt turned and looked at her, his eyes resting on her reddened nose. "Good morning," he replied, "I see that you're in the pink of health."

"Very funny," Alison muttered and wandered over to the refrigerator.

Matt's huge form blocked her way. "Oh, no, you don't—I'm the chef this morning. Now, sit down."

Alison was too surprised to refuse and sat down at the place he indicated at the kitchen table. "But, Matt," she objected weakly, "You don't have to make breakfast."

"Don't complain," he said cheerfully, returning to the stove. "Not everyone gets a breakfast made and served by a Cordon Bleu chef."

"But . . ."

"No buts," he insisted. "How are you feeling?"

"Okay, I guess." Alison grabbed a tissue and sneezed explosively.

Matt glanced at her with sympathy and took the bottle of aspirin off the shelf by his head. He placed them before her with a tall glass of orange juice. "Doctor's orders," he announced. "Take two aspirin and lots of juice. I want you healthy enough to go cross-country skiing when the weather breaks."

Alison was irritated at his domineering tone. "Maybe I don't ski."

"I already checked," he said blithely, ignoring her irritation. "You have a set of cross-country skis on the back porch."

Silenced, Alison sipped the juice and watched Matt as he moved from the stove to the refrigerator and back again. He was obviously very comfortable working in her kitchen and had acquainted himself with every nook and cranny in an amazingly short time. Alison wasn't used to having a man in her house, especially in her kitchen. Even when her parents had lived here, her mother had always done the cooking while her father had prudently stayed away. Alison wasn't so old-fashioned as to believe that cooking was women's work, and she knew that many famous chefs were men; but, on the other hand, she felt distinctly odd, sitting lazily by as Matt, masculine despite the apron and the wooden spoon in his hand, busied himself at the stove.

"There," he announced, sipping from the spoon he had just dipped into a sauce pan. "Just about finished."

"What you you making?"

"Ah-ha," he said mysteriously. "Wouldn't you rather be surprised?"

He grinned boyishly at her and then turned back to the stove. He was clean-shaven and his hair had been roughly combed so that its thick dark waves lay tousled on his forehead. The fact that he was charming and attractive made Alison feel downright cranky. It wasn't fair, she grumbled inwardly, that the man who was her sworn enemy should have turned out to be so personable. It meant that she had to be extraresistant, always on her toes, and very careful never to lose sight of his main objective—the transformation of Fairfax into a resort center.

Then a thought struck her and Alison's eyes widened in shock. Could it be that all of Matt's charming and solicitous behavior was really a deliberate technique on his part to undermine her strong feelings about his proposed resort? That the hot buttered rum of the night before and the Cordon Bleu breakfast this morning were *political* maneuvers? She wouldn't put it past him, she decided grimly, thinking of her evening with him in Key West. Matt Drake was capable of anything. She had no doubt that he would use his personal relationships to further his business ambitions whenever possible.

Matt, completely unaware of her dark thoughts, now turned to her. "Dum-da-da-dum," he announced in a theatrical manner and waved a spatula in the air as if it were a baton. "And now, as a masterpiece of the culinary arts, I present to you"—with a grand flourish he set a plate before her—"eggs Benedict, a combination of toasted muffin, sautéed ham, and a poached egg, all covered in a mouth-watering Hollandaise sauce."

Alison looked down at the plate. She would have liked to throw the eggs Benedict back into Matt's face and let him know that his machinations were useless, but the aroma was delicious. Despite her cold, Alison was starving. She cut off a piece, lifted her fork, and tasted it cautiously. "Very good," she finally admitted with reluctance.

"You are a connoisseur," Matt said bouyantly. "I can see that."

The breakfast was sensational. There was coffee, piping hot, perfectly fried bacon, and—Alison could hardly believe her eyes—freshly baked cinnamon rolls. "How did you manage all this?" she asked, overwhelmed at the spread before her.

"I'm talented," Matt proclaimed modestly as he dug into the food on his plate.

"Hmmm," she grumped.

Matt raised one dark eyebrow. "You don't think so?"

Alison narrowed her eyes at him. "I think you deserve a medal for arrogance," she said with asperity.

Matt only laughed.

The phone that hung on the wall behind Matt's head rang shrilly and he reached out and answered it.

"Hello." He grinned at the surprised squawk at the other end. "Yes, you have the Ramsey residence. Yes, Alison Ramsey does live here."

"Give me the phone!" Alison glared at him and grabbed the receiver that he held out to her. "Hello? Oh, George! How are you—and Karen . . . ?"

"She had a girl, six and a half pounds, at three this morning—both are doing fine." Not even the telephone could conceal the exhaustion evident in George's voice.

"George! How wonderful!" Alison's heart lifted; she

knew how much Karen had wanted a little girl. "When can I come and see them?"

"Karen will probably be ready by tomorrow; she's pretty tired right now."

"You sound like you could use a rest, too," Alison said sympathetically.

"I'm going to sleep at the hospital. I'm snowed in anyway." There was a slight pause. "Alison . . . who answered your telephone?"

"Matt—Martin Drake." She glanced at Matt's grinning face. "He had to spend the night here because of the snow."

"Did you get along all right? Was everything okay?"

"Better than I expected," Alison said. The words held one meaning for George but another for her. For reasons that George knew nothing about, Matt's overnight stay had been less nerve-racking than she had anticipated. She was now crossing her fingers that the rest of his time in Fairfax would be equally placid. "Come for dinner, George," she added.

George's voice was dubious. "I don't think I can. For one thing, I may be snowed in here all day—and for another, Karen's mother is with Jeremy, and I think she has something planned."

"Well, I'll see you tomorrow—and give my love to Karen." After George said goodbye, Alison handed the receiver back to Matt.

"Your friend had her baby?"

Alison nodded and picked up her cup of coffee. "A girl; that's what she wanted."

"How about you, Alison? Do you want to have babies?" His dark head was bent over his plate as he was buttering a cinnamon roll and Alison couldn't see his expression.

"What do you mean?" she asked guardedly.

"Don't you want the usual things that a woman does—marriage and children? This house is very big for one person alone." He was now looking at her seriously and Alison's heart seemed to turn over—some sort of strange reaction to the glint in his dark eyes.

"Someday, maybe—when I meet the right man." She said it hesitantly, but in her tone there was a challenge that Matt didn't hesitate to pick up.

"And what kind of man would that be?"

Alison flushed slightly but answered him steadily. "A man who would make a good husband and father, a man who has principles that he believes in—like honesty and sincerity. Perhaps I sound old-fashioned, but I think a man has to make a commitment—not for one night, or a short-lived affair, but for a lifetime." Alison stopped short and bit her lower lip. She hadn't meant to sound so impassioned.

"I see," Matt murmured, noting the pink flags of color on her cheeks. "And don't any of the local boys fit that bill?"

Alison didn't want him to know that the pickings in Fairfax were slim. "A few are . . . er, interesting."

"But there's no one properly old-fashioned?"

Alison flared up at the note of sarcasm she thought she detected in his voice. "Listen, Matt, I've gone out with plenty of men who think that they're really 'with it' because they're swingers. Each and every one struck me as unhappy and lonely despite his busy social life. And it didn't take me long to realize that all they really wanted was a beautiful woman on their arms or in their b . . ." Alison swallowed and then pushed on, ". . . or in their beds to boost their frail egos."

Matt leaned back in his chair, his arms crossed over his broad chest, and surveyed her angry face. "You sound bitter."

Alison was startled. "Bitter?"

Matt shrugged slightly. "Is antagonistic a better word?"

Alison bristled defensively. "I haven't met a man yet who's proven to me that he's a decent, loving human being instead of"—before she knew it, the word just popped out—"an animal!" Alison was horrified and quickly covered her mouth with one hand. She hadn't meant to say that. She stared at Matt with widened eyes. Didn't that word precisely describe Matt's behavior in Key West? Hadn't he acted like nothing but an animal in pursuit of a night of sex?

"I think I get the picture," Matt said dryly, then stood up and stretched, the broad muscles of his chest straining against the thin fabric of his shirt. Alison hastily looked down at the plate before her, unwilling to be reminded of Matt's potent masculinity.

Suddenly one strong hand was beneath her chin and Matt held her face tilted toward his so that she could not miss the intensity in his dark, gleaming eyes. "Just because a man desires you, Alison, does not make him an animal."

Alison was swimming in the unfathomable depths of his gaze. "I . . . that isn't what I said," she answered a bit wildly. Her senses were reeling at his closeness.

He leaned even closer to her until her whole world seemed to be composed of Matt Drake—of his dark eyes, the sensual curve of his lips, and the breadth of his wide shoulders. "But that's what you meant." He looked at her gravely, and then he spoke in a gentle voice. "You know what I think?"

Wordlessly, she shook her head, her chin still held firmly in his hands.

"I think you're afraid, Alison. Afraid of men—and afraid of sex."

Later, as she stepped onto her skis and bent down to clip on the bindings, Alison had to admit that Matt had touched a raw nerve. She had vehemently denied what he had said, of course, but he had merely smiled enigmatically and walked away. They had not referred to the subject again, but Alison had had plenty of time to think about it. She had spent the morning cleaning the breakfast dishes, making beds, and doing laundry, while Matt had dug out the walkway to the house and made a clearing around the Ferrari. The sun had finally decided to make an appearance and the snowfall had dwindled to nothing. When Matt had suggested a quick lunch and then an outing on skis, Alison had quickly agreed. A breath of fresh air might clear away some of the cobwebs in her mind.

"All set?" Matt stood before her, already clipped into his skis and leaning on his poles. He was dressed in a dark blue form-fitting nylon suit with white racing stripes that ran over his broad shoulders, down his arms, and along the side seams of his pants. The colors enhanced his good looks and the snug fit of the fabric emphasized his every muscle. Alison didn't doubt that Matt had a physique that would make most women go weak in the knees. The fact that he had an equally devastating effect on her made it no easier to bear.

"I'm almost ready," she answered, straightening up. She pulled a pale blue knitted cap onto her head, tucking the loose strands of blond hair under the wool. She felt incredibly amateurish in her heavy white pullover and blue jeans, but then she shrugged. She wasn't, after all, competing with Matt, merely heading off for an afternoon's outing.

"I'll make a track," he said and set off before her. He wore no hat, and his dark hair glinted with mahogany lights in the bright sunlight. The muscles in his legs and thighs pulsed powerfully as he strode forward, setting one ski firmly ahead of the other, and his entire body moved with the grace and coordination of an athlete's.

They skied down the street in front of Alison's house, and the air was crisp but absolutely still. There wasn't a car in sight, and the neighborhood was peaceful except for the occasional roar of a snow blower. Familiar objects had altered overnight into graceful

72

sculptures of white. The trees had acquired foliage of snow, electrical lines looked like party streamers, and even humble garbage pails sported jaunty caps of white. The sky of the morning, dark and cloudy, had turned to an intense turquoise blue, and both Alison and Matt had been forced to put on sunglasses to protect their eyes from the sun's glare as it hit the blanket of snow.

Alison would have enjoyed the whole scene and the invigorating air far more if she could have swept away the thoughts that had plagued her all morning. Had Matt spoken the truth about her? Was she afraid of men and afraid of sex? Her first reaction had been a complete and utter denial; but later, when she was calmer and away from Matt's disturbing presence, his allegation came back to haunt her.

Just a few days before, Karen had said much the same thing—that she treated men like antagonists, as if she were in a perpetual state of war against the opposite sex. Alison had brushed off her comments, but Matt's statement had been like rubbing salt on an open wound. Evidently, somewhere deep inside herself, Alison had known that she was wary of men and the threat that they represented to her peace and tranquillity. Alison could not forget what had happened to her when Matt had kissed her the day before. She had been assaulted and almost overcome by sensations within herself that she had never known existed. She knew, with an absolute certainty, that if he ever touched her again she would succumb to an extent that she did not dare to contemplate. She shivered slightly, less from the briskness of the air than from the cold tenor of her thoughts. The only solution to her problems, she decided, was to stay as far away from Matt as she could. After all, he would be leaving soon, and if she had anything to do about it, they would never cross paths again.

Matt had cut a track down the street, through an

open field, and up to a copse of fir trees that stood on a ridge that overlooked the town. He had stopped to wait for her and was leaning nonchalantly back on his poles, his sunglasses pushed up onto his head, looking more arrogant and self-assured than ever. As she pulled up beside him and planted her poles in the snow, Alison avoided his glance. She had to concede that he had been right in one way—she *was* afraid of him and his aura of intense virility. He seemed to make a mockery of every standard that she had ever set for herself.

Alison looked down at the valley before them, at the shops and houses of Fairfax. The town, glistening with snow, had the appearance of a storybook village.

"Pretty, isn't it?" she ventured, taking a quick glance at Matt's chiseled profile through her lashes.

"Very."

"And so peaceful—and quiet."

Matt turned to her mockingly. "Persistent, aren't you?"

Alison waved at the lovely scene before them. "But it *is* charming, Matt—it doesn't even look like part of the twentieth century."

"And I suppose that's how you prefer it."

"I . . . yes, I do."

Matt glanced at her defiant expression. "That's your problem, Alison; you want to live in another era. You should take a good, long look at Fairfax. It may look pretty from here, but I know what that town looks like from Main Street—old, dingy, and outdated. Almost every building needs repair."

"How can you say that?" Alison protested. "The pharmacy just had a new front put on."

"That's just one instance and you know it. Very few of the businessmen have enough money to fix up their property. The farmers around Fairfax have been selling out at a constant rate, and soon there won't be any reason for the town to exist at all."

"That's not true!"

Matt looked down at her and his tone was hard. "You're living in some kind of dream world, Alison, where financial and economic concerns don't exist. But Fairfax isn't in that dream world; it isn't going to survive the twentieth century unless some new industry settles in and makes the town a viable place to live. Fairfax needs money, taxes from thriving businesses, and a well-to-do population."

"What makes you think that you know what's best for Fairfax?" Alison flared up. "You didn't even grow up here—you're a stranger!"

"You're too close to the problem," Matt countered, "and can't see the forest for the trees. Alison, Fairfax is dying and you're helping to bury it." His voice was cold and clipped, and Alison had a faint inkling of the cool rationality that Matt brought to his own business.

Still, she protested. "Not everyone agrees with you, Matt. I did get voted onto the town council."

"Yes, under Fairfax's voting regulations."

Alison, puzzled, turned to look at Matt. He was glancing at the scene before him, and she could read nothing from his enigmatic expression.

"What are you implying?" she asked coldly.

"Since the five council members are chosen from a list of candidates by the number of votes each wins, it's not unlikely that one or two may represent only a minority's interests."

Alison tossed her head. "Don't you believe that minorities have a right to be represented, or are you too elitist?"

Matt ignored the barb and went implacably on. "The most popular councilman won with eighty-five hundred votes. You squeaked in with only three hundred ninety."

"How . . . how did you know that?"

"Because someone else told me about it."

"The mayor?" Alison snorted. "He's the most partisan, narrow-minded politician in upstate New York—you'll never get an unbiased opinion from him."

Matt's voice was quiet. "No, it wasn't the mayor."

Alison looked down suddenly at the tips of her skis. Something in his tone told her that she wasn't going to like the answer to her next question. "Who told you?"

"George."

"George! How could . . . why did . . ." Alison was appalled.

"When I spoke to him on the phone before coming here he gave me a rundown on the political situation."

"But George . . . of all people . . ." Alison felt betrayed, as if she had been stabbed in the back when she least expected it. She had known that George's feelings about the resort had not exactly matched her own, but she had never suspected that they might be diametrically opposed, or that he would aid and abet her greatest enemy.

Matt pulled off a glove and ran long fingers through his dark hair. "You shouldn't be surprised at George; after all, he's a businessman. He has to stake his future on the continued existence of Fairfax."

"Well, he's only one man and one opinion," she said with more bravado than she felt.

"That may be so, but I think there are a lot of others who share his views."

Alison felt helpless in the face of Matt's calm and cold logic and it made her furious. "The people of Fairfax," she spat out at him, lifting one pole and jamming it back into the snow for emphasis, "don't want you, your resort, *or* your business!"

"Ah, but they do."

"Hah!" She glared at him.

His dark eyes mocked her. "How do you think I picked Fairfax, Alison? Do you think that I threw a dart at a map of the United States and decided to build a resort wherever it landed? The Businessmen's Association of Fairfax wrote to me, asking me to look into the possibility of building here. I said that I was interested, and when the Derrick farm came on the market, they told me it would be perfect."

Alison looked away from him, from the cold glint in his eye and the arrogant line of his jaw. She looked down at Fairfax below them. The stores, the streets, and the white-spired church blurred before her eyes. "I see," she said helplessly, swallowing hard and fighting the tears that threatened to spill over. "Now I understand."

That evening, Alison sat before the roaring fire that Matt had built in the fireplace and sipped at her mug of hot coffee. She felt depressed, upset, confused, and on edge. The things that Matt had told her, plus the continued fact of his presence, had made the last twenty-four hours the worst in Alison's life. He had taught her things she hadn't known about her own hometown and things that she hadn't known about herself. None of these revelations had turned out to be pleasant.

Not even the sound of the snowplows working their way up her street cheered her up. Alison knew that Matt planned to leave extremely early the next morning for a two-week holiday, skiing in Canada. He had told her that there was no need for her to get up early and say goodbye, and Alison had, with some difficulty, restrained herself from making the retort that had sprung to her lips. He couldn't leave soon enough for her.

Alison looked around the quiet living room, at Samson curled up in a chair, at the reflection of the orange flames in the gleaming wood of the coffee table, and wished that she could feel as serene as her surroundings. She sniffed slightly and pulled a tissue from the pocket of her slacks. Her cold had not developed with the rapidity that she had expected, and it seemed that an afternoon in the cold air had even been medicinal. She leaned back, placing her coffee on the table beside her, and put her stockinged feet up on the ottoman, determined to relax and be at ease when Matt came down after showering.

If Alison had not been so infuriated with him she would have enjoyed having a man around the house. He had refused a big dinner, quickly eaten a sandwich, and spent several hours clearing the snow from the long driveway that led up to her garage and chopping wood for the fire. It was obvious that Matt was as proficient in the outdoors as he was at his business. She knew that, without him, her car would have remained in the garage until the snow melted, a friendly neighbor had offered his services or the man from the local garage had been free.

A noise made her turn and Alison saw Matt in the doorway, tucking his shirt casually into his slacks. "How's the fire?" he asked and walked over to the fireplace. He took the poker and idly rearranged the glowing logs.

"Burning," Alison answered idiotically. She could not think one single coherent thought after seeing him in the doorway. He had changed into black slacks that fit, Alison noted with a feeling of faintness, almost like a second skin, and he had left his long-sleeved black shirt open almost to his belt line, revealing a triangle of brown skin and coarse black hair. The sight of his bared chest brought back, in almost Technicolor vividness, the end of that evening in Key West when he had appeared in the bedroom, almost nude, every muscle gleaming in the lamplight.

Alison rubbed her hand across her eyes as if to erase the sight of Matt from her mind. When she brought her hand down she discovered that he was now standing before her, his hands on his hips and his legs astride, like some sort of colossus. "You don't look well," he said solicitously. "Is your cold bothering you?"

Alison knew that she didn't look well. She had felt the blood draining from her cheeks. "Uh . . . no . . . I mean, I'm not sure." Alison stumbled over her words. The closer Matt came, the more she felt like jumping up, dashing upstairs, and hiding in a closet. Dressed all in black with his dark skin, eyes, and hair, he resembled the devil, come to offer her temptations that she could never resist. The lights that seemed to flare in his eyes as he looked down at her made her shiver.

"You're cold."

"No! No, I'm not."

But it was too late. Matt sat down on the couch next to her and threw his arm along the back of the sofa. He scrutinized her face. "A minute ago you were pale and now you're flushed." He paused for a moment, eying her mockingly. "Is something the matter?"

Alison ran a shaky hand through her blond hair, stared straight ahead, and flushed even pinker. How could she tell Matt that there was only one thing bothering her and that that was his undeniably virile body? Even she could hardly believe that a mere assortment of arms, legs, and a torso could be so . . . so distracting!

His hand moved from the back of the sofa to the nape of her neck and he began to slowly caress the sensitive skin under her hair. Alison felt a sweet shiver run down her spine and her heart began to race like that of a wild animal who was being hunted. Now that he was only inches away she could feel the warmth of his body and smell his clean masculine scent. Alison didn't dare to look at him and tried to move away.

"You *are* afraid of men," he murmured, his fingers playing in the thick strands of her hair.

"No," she whispered and tried again to move away, but this time he pinioned her wrist with his other hand.

"Then why are you trembling?" The hand at her neck now moved around until he had hold of her chin and could force her to look at him. Alison felt as if she were drowning in the deep and glinting depths of his eyes.

"I . . . I don't know," she whispered.

He let go of her chin and traced her parted lips with one finger. "Do you know the best way to cure a phobia?" he asked conversationally.

"No." Alison barely mouthed the word and her eyes dropped from his face to the open triangle of his shirt, where his skin gleamed like highly polished bronze. She had the insane desire to run her fingers through the hair on his chest. Quickly, she looked back up again.

His mouth quirked slightly. "The best method of curing a fear is to confront it." The hand that was now moving from the corners of her mouth over her cheek to her earlobe belied the clinical tone of his voice.

"Matt . . ." she said feebly, but her protestation came too late. He had already pulled her closer with arms that felt like iron and the touch of his mouth effectively silenced her.

If his kiss had been hard or brutal or painful Alison would have had something to struggle against, to fight with all her might. But his softness undermined every defense that she had constructed and she yielded to the play of his lips on hers, to the tongue that parted her teeth and invaded her mouth with a warmth and sweetness that she had never conceived of as possible.

Of their own accord her arms rose to encircle his neck and her fingers luxuriated in the thickness of his hair. She was being carried along on a sweet tide of desire and every scruple and standard that she had prized was swept away in its rush. It seemed that all her life Alison had been waiting for this moment and her body reacted as if it had a will of its own. Her slim form arched against his taut, lean body and she gloried in the feel of her breasts, bare beneath her thin shirt, pressed against the hardness of his chest.

She made no protest when, wordlessly, he pulled her

down onto the rug before the fire, and she did nothing but moan when he leaned over, pinning her down with his thigh and burying his face in her hair. He placed soft butterfly kisses under her ear, down her neck, and onto the shoulder blade that was exposed by the open collar of her blouse.

Then he raised his head and the fire lit his lean, dark face. Alison's arms tightened around his chest at his expression. Then he kissed her again, and this time the kiss was wild and passionate. Alison felt herself melting . . . drowning . . . sinking. . . . When his hand opened the buttons of her shirt she felt only a delicious anticipation, and the warmth of his hand cupping her breast and the sensation created by his finger brushing her erect nipple were exquisite.

She had pulled his shirt out from his pants and was running her hands over the muscles that rippled beneath the warm skin of his back when Alison felt Matt's fingers at the waist band of her slacks. She stiffened, and Matt's hand immediately stopped moving. He raised his head and looked down at her silently, at her flushed face and at the swelling roundness of her bared breasts, all bathed in the rosy glow of the fire.

"Well?"

"I . . . please stop."

Do you usually play these games with the men of your choice?" His voice was harsh, and Alison cringed.

"No," she whispered. How could she tell him that no man had ever touched her that way? That she had given him, of her body, far more than she had given to anyone else? In this day and age, her purity was considered laughable, and Alison could not bear the thought of Matt laughing at her. Not again.

Matt rolled off her. "Am I a special case?" he asked sarcastically.

Alison sat up and buttoned her blouse with shaking fingers. Matt was leaning on one elbow, his long legs stretched before him, and Alison hastily looked away from the evidence of his arousal. "I . . . I don't think it's . . . well, ethical."

"Ethical?" Matt was astounded.

"We're political opponents." Her argument sounded clumsy even to her own ears. She tried to comb the tangles out of her hair with her fingers.

"My dear," Matt drawled, "don't you know that politics makes strange bedfellows?" He stopped and Alison got the full impact of the quote.

She flinched. "You're twisting my meaning."

Matt stood up, jammed his hands into his pockets, and looked down at her bent head. "Then the next time you go in for such political strategy, let me know. Now that we're opponents, I won't be so . . . polite," he said derisively.

Alison burned with indignation. She stood up quickly and faced him. "I wouldn't consider you polite under any circumstances," she hissed at him.

"Just what are you implying?" His voice was low and ominous.

Alison ignored the threat. "Is it polite to . . . to hire call girls?"

"Call girls?"

"Isn't that what you had planned in Key West? A night with a call girl?"

"I don't suppose you'd believe . . ." Matt frowned and surveyed Alison, her slim body taut with anger. He shook his head. "No, I don't suppose you would," he murmured.

Alison clenched her teeth. "Don't try to deny it."

Matt leaned nonchalantly against the mantelpiece and eyed her slowly from head to toe. "So, you think I'm the kind of man who has to resort to call girls, do you?" His voice positively purred.

"Aren't you?" Alison lifted her chin defiantly.

This time she screamed when he grabbed her and forced her into his arms. His kiss was brutal and insistent, and Alison found that she was helpless against the strength with which he held her head, against the powerful thrust of his body as he forced her hips against his. Then his touch changed from masterful to gentle, from harsh to sweet, and Alison felt a seductive warmth steal over her senses. At the exact moment that she yielded, her body rising urgently toward his, Matt let her go and stepped back.

He gazed at the softness of her parted lips and the luminosity in her wide blue-green eyes. "You have a lot to learn about men," he said harshly, "if you think that I need to hire call girls." And, turning his back to her, Matt strode out of the room.

Chapter Five

Alison sat before her desk at the radio station and nibbled desultorily on her ham sandwich. She had had little appetite during the past two weeks, and even her friends had noticed that her already slim form was becoming even slimmer. Alison put the sandwich back in its wrapper and stared despondently before her. Ever since Matt's precipitate arrival in her life nothing had gone right and no one had behaved normally. Every belief that Alison held about herself, her friends, and her hometown had been toppled or turned topsy-turvy.

It hadn't taken much snooping on her part to find out that Matt had been accurate about the Businessmen's Association. They had met secretly about a year before and had petitioned Matt's firm to look into the potential of Fairfax as a resort center. When the Derrick farm had gone on the market they had suggested that it would make the ideal property, and Matt, flying into Fairfax for a few hours, had bought it.

George, of course, had known all along. When she confronted him with the evidence he had argued along a simple line of logic. Fairfax was going into a decline, and if efforts were not made to bring new industry to the area it was going to disappear—and his radio station along with it.

"But why didn't you say something to me?" Alison had wailed.

"Because I knew that you wouldn't agree no matter what I said," George had replied. "You were bound and determined to stick to your ideas and wouldn't listen to anyone who disagreed with you. Remember that party we had for Karen's birthday last year?" Alison nodded. "I tried to tell you then, but you were too stubborn to listen."

And when Alison thought back to that party she remembered a conversation she had had with George, Lillian Scott, the town beautician, and Tom Berke, who owned Fairfax's only restaurant. When they had started to discuss the possibilities of bringing a resort to Fairfax she had walked away in anger. George was right; she had never wanted to listen to anyone whose opinions differed from hers.

Karen had been even more blunt. "You were born with that Ramsey pride and you see everything in terms of black and white."

They had been having coffee on a Sunday afternoon. George had taken Jeremy sledding, and the new baby, Carrie, was sleeping in her crib upstairs. Karen was leaning back in the armchair with her eyes closed and her face weary. Carrie had turned out to be a good baby, but Alison knew that coping with both a newborn and a two-year-old was tiring.

"I still don't want to see Fairfax turn into a tourist trap." Alison placed her emptied coffee cup on the end table beside the couch.

"That's fine, you're entitled to your opinion; but it seems to me that there's plenty of room for compromise. The resort *could* be tasteful—we won't know until we see the plans at the town meeting."

Alison was firm. "I'm still going to fight it."

Karen opened her eyes and glanced at her friend. "And Matt Drake, too?" Alison had given her an expurgated version of Matt's overnight stay during the blizzard, but, as a close friend, Karen had perceptively seen far more than she had been told.

"He's aggressive and chauvinistic."

"Well, I think he sounds charming—he dug you out, made you a gourmet breakfast, took you skiing; and Violet Stacey"—Karen named a widow who lived in the house behind Alison's—"tells me that he's very handsome."

Alison looked up quickly from her contemplation of her nails. "How would she know?"

"She saw him chopping wood." Karen smiled at Alison's grimace of disgust. "You know small towns."

Unfortunately, Alison did. The news about her male guest was soon going to be common knowledge. "Drat," she muttered.

Karen grinned. "It's going to ruin your reputation," she teased.

"Matt and I have absolutely nothing in common."

Karen had looked at her with disbelief. Alison had always been blithely contemptuous of the men she had dated, but never so adamant about disliking them. Karen had the strong suspicion that Matt Drake had been a little more than Alison could handle. "He didn't attract you at all?" she probed gently.

Alison looked at Karen's sympathetic expression. She would have liked to pour all her confusion and bewilderment out to her friend, but a certain shyness held her back. How could she ever explain to Karen, already a married woman and mother, the emotional turmoil that she had experienced during and after her encounter with Matt? "Not in the least," she had said firmly.

Alison heaved a great sigh and put her half-eaten lunch into her desk drawer. Maybe she'd be hungry later on in the day, although she doubted it. She had suffered the tortures of the damned ever since Matt's departure two weeks before. She hadn't seen him again after he had left the living room, and he had, as promised, left in the morning long before she had gotten up. A short thank-you note had been left on the kitchen table, written in a thick, decisive script.

She had relived, over and over again, those moments she had spent in his arms, and each time she cringed at the way her physical desires had conquered her moral standards. How could she have allowed him to touch her in that intimate way? And given him the right to think that she would be willing to go farther? But no matter which way she examined the events of that evening, Alison ended up blaming herself. She could have held him off—she could have pushed him away. But she hadn't; she had willingly—and even eagerly—entered his arms. No wonder he had been angry when she had retreated. Nothing in her actions had given him the slightest hint that she was going to refuse his ultimate advances.

Still, Alison held firmly to the belief that such intimacies belonged to love, to marriage, and to an enduring relationship. That was why she despised Matt—a man who used women, who believed that sex could be bought as if it were a casual purchase. No matter how witty, charming, or sexy Matt was, Alison could never forget that he had planned to sleep with her as if she were a . . . a prostitute. And when she thought of his experience and evident skill and the way she had yielded, Alison blushed with shame. A man like that would never be able to understand her feelings, her standards. If ever their paths crossed again—and Alison fervently hoped that they wouldn't—Matt Drake was going to receive the brush-off of his lifetime. She would teach him to tangle with Alison Ramsey!

Determined to forget Matt Drake, Alison pulled a box of reel-to-reel tapes from the shelf behind her head and brought them into the room that had the splicing machine. One of the free-lance journalists had conducted a series of interviews with the local representative to the state legislature and it was Alison's job to edit the tapes into one cohesive interview that could be played on the next day's evening talk show. She knew from long experience that she would spend several hours trying to edit out every hum and haw and every inane statement. Resignedly, she sat down before the machine and placed the first tape on the turntable. She pressed the play button, and the reel slowly turned. *Your opponents,* the tape began, *have called your system of tax reform cumbersome and inefficient. How does this statement affect* . . . The voice droned on and on, and almost five minutes passed before Alison realized that she wasn't even listening. Come on, she prodded herself, you can't think of Matt Drake forever. Now, get to work.

Two hours later, after she had thrown her sweater to the floor, haphazardly rolled up the sleeves of her blouse, and ruined a perfectly good hairdo by running her fingers wildly through her hair, Alison decided that she had finally managed to compress the interviews into the required eight minutes and seventeen seconds. She rewound the spliced tape, then stood up and paced as she listened to the entire piece again. She no longer even heard the words; she was now listening intently to the rhythm of the voices and background sounds of the tape. She stopped suddenly as an earsplitting whine came from the machine, indicating an unsuccessful splice.

Just as she was gritting her teeth and steeling herself to face the repair job the receptionist buzzed her. Alison ran back to her office and picked up the phone.

"Hi, how's your sanity this afternoon?" the receptionist's voice sounded in her ear.

"Lousy; why?"

"Mr. Beecham's on the line."

Alison gave a dramatic groan. Mr. Beecham was a retired farmer who was active in local events and kept up eagerly with the Fairfax news. He didn't hesitate for a minute to put in his two cents if he felt criticism was due, and he frequently called the radio station if he thought it had been remiss in reporting local news. It was one of Alison's less enjoyable jobs to handle Mr. Beecham.

"Okay." She sighed. "I think I'm ready. Put him on."

It took her ten minutes to smooth Mr. Beecham's ruffled feathers. The radio station, it seemed, had neglected to announce a meeting of the Horticulturist Society, of which Mr. Beecham was a member. And the fact that it *had* reported news about the rival Nature Club had not helped matters at all. Alison tactfully reminded Mr. Beecham that the radio station required all local associations to send in their news before the event occurred and then they would be guaranteed coverage. The phone squawked and sputtered. Mr. Beecham, she realized with a sinking heart, expected the radio station to read minds. By the time she had gracefully conceded defeat and promised him that there wouldn't be a second failure, Alison's head had begun to pound unbearably. When she hung up she folded her arms before her and placed her head on them, closing her eyes. Was this day ever going to end? she thought miserably.

"Sleeping on the job?"

Alison brought her head up quickly and then had the overwhelming urge to lay it down again. Matt Drake stood in the doorway of her office, leaning against the frame, tall and lean in a denim jacket and jeans. Alison's first thought was that she had forgotten just how handsome he was. Her second thought wouldn't have borne repeating in general company.

"What are you doing here?" she asked as coldly as she could.

"Driving back from Canada to New York City. I thought I'd stop in and in exchange for your . . . er, delightful hospitality take you out to dinner."

Alison took a deep breath. "You thought wrong."

Matt deliberately mistook her meaning. "Not hungry?"

"As a matter of fact, I'm not."

"You look like you could use a good meal."

Alison flushed as his eyes ran over the thinning contours of her face. "That wasn't what I meant," she said nervously, anxiously trying to comb out the tangles in her hair with her fingers. "I have absolutely no intention of . . ."

". . . going out with me." He completed the sentence for her with a grin on his tanned face. Her rejection, she saw with outrage, only seemed to give him cause for amusement.

"That's right," she said curtly. "Now, will you please—"

Matt uncurled himself from the doorway and interrupted. "I don't suppose I could bribe you?" he said smoothly.

Alison eyed him warily. "What do you mean?"

"There is a certain blueprint . . ." He left the words hanging in the air between them.

Alison stood up quickly. "What blueprint?"

"The blueprint of the . . ." He looked at her and shook his head. "No, I don't suppose you'd be interested."

"Do you have the blueprint for the resort with you?" she asked with incredulity, barely noticing the sensual way his eyes ran over the smooth fit of her blue blouse and matching straight skirt.

He shook his head in mock admiration. "Brilliant, a brilliant deduction."

The thought of the blueprint made Alison's fingers twitch. She was dying to get her hands on those plans. "I would love to . . ." she said quickly, then paused.

". . . come to dinner with me." His dark eyes glinted at her.

"That's despicable—it's out-and-out bribery!" Alison sputtered.

Matt shrugged his broad shoulders and started to walk away. "Perhaps the mayor would prefer an invitation to dinner," he said over his shoulder.

For one second Alison stood frozen by her desk. She had never met any man so annoying or exasperating or . . . Suddenly she realized that he truly intended to leave. She ran to the doorway. "Matt!"

He turned and looked at her. "Yes?"

"I—" She had no chance to finish her sentence as George turned the corner into the hallway and almost collided with Matt.

"Excuse me; I didn't see . . ." George glanced at Alison's flushed face and then eyed Matt curiously. "Is anything the matter, Alison?"

Alison opened her mouth to let George know what a skunk Matt was and then closed it again. The wicked gleam in Matt's eyes reminded her that he was capable of twisting anything she said into a form beneficial to himself. Sullenly, she introduced the two men and gritted her teeth at George's warm welcome.

"You must come to dinner tonight," he said impulsively after shaking Matt's hand. "I'll give my wife a call and—"

"George!" Alison said, admonishingly. "You know Karen is too tired from the baby to have last-minute company."

George hesitated and rubbed one hand across his forehead in a weary gesture. Alison suddenly realized that having a two-and-a-half-week old infant in the house was just as draining for George as for Karen. "You're right," he said slowly and then brightened. "But you were coming for dinner anyway, Alison; you can help Karen rustle something up. It doesn't have to be fancy."

Matt interrupted Alison's objection. "Look, it doesn't seem like a good time to—"

George's voice was firm. "Of course you're going to come. Alison was coming anyway and she's going to baby-sit Jeremy afterward while Karen and I take the baby to the clinic—she has a bad rash and . . ." He looked at Matt with apology and laughed ruefully. "Forget it—what a bachelor doesn't know won't keep him up nights."

Matt smiled at George with sympathy. "It's murder, I know; when my niece was born she had a set of lungs that could put a fishwife to shame."

Alison looked back and forth at the two men, grinning in camaraderie, and cursed silently. If she wasn't mistaken, Matt was going to charm the pants off George. No one would ever believe that underneath he was conniving, nasty, and dominating.

"Come to dinner, Matt, and keep Alison company while she takes care of Jeremy."

Alison stared in openmouthed astonishment at George's suggestion. How could he? He knew that Matt upset her and disturbed her. He knew that the last thing in the world she wanted was to spend even one second in Matt's infuriating company. "Oh, no," she said faintly, "that won't be necessary."

Matt's grin indicated that he knew exactly what she was thinking, but his words to George showed that he didn't care in the least. "Sounds good to me."

"Fine, that's settled." George ran a distracted hand over his hair. "Look, will you excuse me for a while? I have to get this evening's program sorted out before I go home. Alison, call Karen and make some arrangements, will you? I'll see everyone later." And, saying a quick goodbye, he walked past Alison and into his office.

After George had closed the door Alison glared at Matt. If looks could have killed he would have been resting six feet under. "I don't know how you do it," she muttered, her lips pressed together in anger.

"I told you I was talented," he said mockingly.

Alison placed her hands on her hips. "What about the blueprint?"

"What blueprint?" he said, affecting an air of innocence.

"You said I could see the blueprint if I agreed to have dinner with you."

"But you *didn't* agree to have dinner with me," he pointed out.

Alison saw red. "Why, you lousy, conniving . . ."

"Tch, tch; aren't you letting your temper get the better of you?"

"I wish you'd get out of my life," she hissed.

"Take it easy, sweetheart," he said in a voice that dripped with false sympathy. "You'll only have to endure a few more hours of my company. I'll pick you up at five." And he turned on his heel and strode away.

As Alison watched his broad back retreat her shoulders slumped and her forgotten headache renewed its pounding with a vengeance. Her every encounter with Matt seemed to turn into a personal defeat. Still, there was a chance that their evening with George and Karen would not be so traumatic. After all, they would be chaperones, even if they weren't aware of it, and Alison prayed that Jeremy could be kept up later than usual. Surely even a determined man like Matt wouldn't try anything in the presence of a child.

Alison grumbled to herself as she cut the chocolate cake into squares and took the coffeepot off the stove. Matt's visit to the Birches had been wildly successful and Alison would have liked to wring his charming neck. As a guest, his manners were impeccable. He had picked Alison up promptly at five and his Ferrari had been loaded with packages. There was wine for dinner, a bottle of aperitif for later, toys for Jeremy and Carrie, and two packages for Karen. One had been the latest best-seller, and the other a cut-glass bottle of very expensive French perfume. Matt had handed them to Karen, saying simply that, in his experience, mothers of new babies liked to be reminded both that they had intellectual interests and that they were women. From Karen's delighted exclamations Alison surmised that he was right, and she was surprised at his perceptiveness. Most men, she realized, were considerably less sensitive.

He had talked knowledgeably about the radio business with George as Karen and Alison had put together a quick meal. He had been absolutely delightful with Jeremy after the Birches had taken Carrie to the clinic and Alison had cleaned up the dinner dishes. And all evening he had been kind and attentive to a tired Karen, who had responded with more smiles and chatter than Alison had seen in months. The long pregnancy and then the care of a small infant, Alison realized, had made Karen hungry for company. And now that Karen and George were back and the children were in bed, Alison could hear laughter coming from the dining room where Matt was entertaining them with jokes.

Alison slammed a tray down on the kitchen counter and placed some cups on it. She knew that she should be pleased that the evening had gone so well and that George and Karen were having such a good time, but Matt's success made her positively irritable. It made everything she had said about him to Karen look like a pack of lies.

Alison felt an arm slip around her waist and looked to see Karen standing beside her. "Oh, Alison," she breathed, "he is *so* nice." Karen hugged her briefly and then began to gather some cake forks and spoons.

"He is *not* nice," Alison muttered, glowering.

Karen ignored her. "And so handsome. Alison—what a catch!"

She was about to go on in that enthusiastic vein when Alison stopped her in alarm. "Wait a minute, Karen—he's not my 'catch' at all."

Karen smiled at her. "You must be blind, then.

94

Don't you see the look in his eyes whenever you're around? I'm so excited for you!"

"That look," Alison said, her teeth clenched, "has absolutely nothing to do with affection. Matt is only interested in me from a . . . a physical point of view."

Karen glanced at Alison's pink cheeks. "And what's wrong with that?" she asked gently.

"Don't you think . . . Karen, how can you say that?" Alison stared at her friend. Karen was the last person she would have suspected of being sympathetic to Matt Drake.

"Most men who are in love are interested in physical attraction—it's only normal."

"Love!" Alison said in utter disbelief. "Who said anything about love?"

"You may be wearing blinkers, Alison, but I'm not. That man loves you even if he doesn't know it yet."

"You're crazy—absolutely crazy."

"Alison, listen to me." Karen put down the creamer she was holding and faced Alison with determination. "Matt Drake is the most interesting and gorgeous man who's ever come into your life and *you're* the one who's crazy if you let him go."

"Let him go? You must be kidding! I don't ever want to see him again!"

"You once told me that if the right man ever came along you'd know him in an instant. Well, if Matt isn't that man, then my name isn't Karen Birch."

"He's not right for me," Alison protested. "He's arrogant and overbearing and . . ."

". . . and handsome, intelligent, and very sexy. Would you rather have some meek little pushover? Matt is not only just right for you," Karen said triumphantly, "but I think, Alison, that you've finally met your match."

As the four of them had their coffee and cake, Alison was subdued, trying to digest Karen's words. She glanced surreptitiously through her lashes at Matt more than once. Karen was right in one way—he *was* handsome and he *was* sexy. His midnight-blue suit revealed, rather than concealed, his muscular physique, and the color enhanced his striking dark looks.

But surely Karen couldn't have been right about the rest, not when she had said that Matt loved her. That was absolutely ridiculous. Would a man who loved her subject her to such embraces? Would he treat her as a sex object? Would he mock her as Matt had done? As she sipped her coffee Alison pondered the question and then came to her conclusion. Of course not; the man who loved her would respect her values, her standards, and her person. He would be supportive and understanding, not disturbing and insensitive to her feelings. And he wouldn't use call girls.

". . . Actually, I did bring along a blueprint, a sketch of the outside of the main building, really."

Alison had been so deeply immersed in her thoughts that she had missed a part of their conversation, but the word "blueprint" snared her attention and she looked up to catch Matt's mocking glance.

"Can we see it?" Karen asked.

"It's right here." Matt reached into the enormous bag that had held all the gifts and pulled out a cardboard cylinder. As Karen and Alison cleared the table of cups and plates he laid the roll of paper out before them, holding it open with his hands.

Alison and the Birches all eagerly leaned over it. It was the architect's rendering of the front of the main lodge, a sprawling stone building with a curved driveway that blended in with the surrounding trees and the rolling hills behind it.

One tree caught Alison's eye. "Why, that's the big oak tree!" she exclaimed. There was one tree on the Derrick property that was widely considered to be the oldest in the county. It was enormous in its girth and had served generations of farm children as the perfect site for tree houses and swings.

"I wanted to keep the landscaping around the buildings as natural as possible," Matt explained. "A tree like that should never be cut down."

George was impressed. "It really looks very attractive."

Matt stood and rolled the sketch up. "The building should suit the property. It should look as if it has been part of the scenery for years instead of being a new structure."

"What's going to be inside?" Karen asked as she brought out the wineglasses for the aperitif.

"A large central room with a big stone fireplace, a card room, two dining areas, an indoor pool, a library, a stationery shop—perhaps a separate cocktail lounge."

"Do you have blueprints for the interior as well?" George pulled the stopper from the aperitif bottle and began to pour the golden liqueur.

"Yes, but they're in my main office in Key West."

"It sure would be interesting to see the rest," George said as he handed a glass to Matt.

"I'm sorry that I couldn't bring them," Matt said apologetically, "but they're still being worked on."

"George," Karen said, and something in her voice made Alison look up from her contemplation of the glass in her hand, "wouldn't it be a good idea for the radio station to report on Matt's concept of the resort?"

George acknowledged her statement. "Yes, it could be."

Karen drummed her fingernails on the table. "You know . . . an investigation that would tell the people what the resort would look like, how suitable it would be, the facilities—that sort of thing."

"You mean send a reporter down?" Matt asked.

Alison looked quickly from Matt to Karen. She was beginning to have a faint inkling of what Karen was up to and she stiffened.

Karen grabbed on to Matt's words. "That's it," she said eagerly and turned to George. "Send someone from Fairfax to Key West to interview Matt and the architects."

"Hmmm." George pondered the thought. "That could be interesting."

Matt leaned back in his chair and smiled at Karen. "That's a very clever idea. I'll have to send the blueprints here for the town council anyway, but this would give the residents a preview."

Karen was now bubbling with enthusiasm and Alison waited tensely to hear her next words. "And I know the perfect person to send," she announced.

George looked up. "Who?"

"Alison," Karen said triumphantly and cast a conspiratorial look at Matt. Alison could have sworn that he winked back at her.

"No!" Alison stood up quickly, staring at Karen in disbelief and almost upsetting the table. "No! Not me—I'm not the right person at all."

Matt swirled the liqueur in its glass. "Oh?" he asked. "Why not?"

You know all too well why not, her eyes shot back at him, but instead of saying so, she groped to find a good reason. "Because I . . . I'm opposed to it. My opinions would be worthless. I'm not impartial," she finally said desperately.

George struck the next blow. "You might be perfect," he said reflectively. "Everyone in Fairfax knows how you feel. If you find something positive to say about the resort, then we'll know it's good."

"That's crazy!" she protested. "If I *don't* say anything positive, then everyone will think it's because I'm biased." She glanced wildly at the three of them. Karen looked smug, Matt's lips were quirked into a sardonic smile, and George appeared to be unconvinced.

"I don't think so," he said after a pause. "It will give an interesting slant to the whole business."

Alison switched tactics. "But it's too expensive. The station's budget couldn't expand to meet the expense of the trip and the accommodations."

George rubbed his jaw and looked at Karen. "Our condominium is rented for the next few months, isn't it?"

Karen nodded reluctantly, and Alison had a faint gleam of hope. Matt's next words dashed it. "She could stay at the Hotel Amérique for nothing. After all, I own it, and besides, that's where my main offices are."

Karen looked like the cat who had found the cream. "Well, that settles it, then."

"Oh, no, it doesn't," Alison objected with a deep, shaky breath. "Not even wild horses—"

"There's another angle that might be interesting," Matt interrupted smoothly and turned to George. "Alison could give us some input on the plans. They're not finalized, and we'd appreciate her criticisms, or"—and he slightly inclined his dark head in her direction—"her praise."

They all looked at Alison as she abruptly sat down. She knew when she was defeated. The investigation of the resort was a plum job and she'd have to be mad to pass it up. And the clincher was Matt's offer to give her the opportunity to influence his decision. There was a good chance that the plans for the resort would be passed by the town council, and she knew that she would feel considerably better about the whole thing if she were involved in the planning.

"All right," she said with reluctance. "I'll go." She looked down into her golden drink, knowing that she would not be able to bear the triumph gleaming in Matt's eyes.

Karen all but clapped her hands in delight. "That's wonderful! I just know that Alison will do a terrific job; don't you, Matt?"

"Yes, terrific," he replied, and Alison knew that she was the only person in the room who had caught the note of mockery beneath the composure in his voice.

Matt drove Alison home not too much later and neither of them spoke for the short distance. Alison was deep in thoughts of revenge and despair. She could kill Karen, she really could. How could her best friend do something like that to her? Alison felt like a sacrificial victim placed on the altar of Karen's matchmaking ambitions. She should have known that Karen would try something sneaky to throw her into Matt's arms. After all, she and George had been trying to find a man for Alison for years.

Matt, no doubt, felt both smug and triumphant. She glanced at his strong hands on the wheel of the Ferrari. Alison was sure that he was accustomed to getting just what he wanted, and she knew only too well what that was: Alison Ramsey in his bed. She scoffed at Karen's talk of love. Karen didn't know Matt and didn't know the way he had tried to seduce her the night after the blizzard. Alison now regretted her reluctance to tell Karen what had happened. If she had done so, she wouldn't have found herself facing a trip to Key West and several days in Matt's unsettling presence.

Matt stopped the car before her house and waited, his profile strong and mysterious in the dim light cast by the streetlamps.

"Aren't you staying in Fairfax?" Alison asked, feeling strangely hesitant to get out of the car.

Matt turned to her and the lights caught in his hair, turning it into a metallic, gleaming dark helmet. "I'm driving to New York tonight. I have a business meeting first thing in the morning."

"Oh," Alison said. She had wondered where he had

100

intended to stay during the night and had planned on cutting him dead if he asked to spend another night in her guest room.

"You sound disappointed," he said curiously, as he leaned toward her.

"Uh . . . I'm not." Alison stumbled over the words. "I mean, I was just wondering . . ."

Her words were silenced by the soft brush of his mouth against hers. "That's all right," he said gently as he pulled away. "You're going to see lots more of me in Key West than you bargained for." Matt reached over her lap and, flipping up the handle, pushed open the door. "Good night, Alison."

Matt was already pulling away from the curb with a powerful roar when Alison came to her senses and found that she was standing on the sidewalk, one hand against her lips. How was she going to cope with Matt Drake? she wondered with a hopeless feeling. She never knew what to expect from him. One minute he was forceful and arrogant; the next he treated her with an almost gentle indifference. She wasn't sure what she had expected from him in the car, but it hadn't been a quick kiss and that brief goodbye.

Alison trudged up the path to her house and fumbled in her purse for the key. Why was she feeling so let down? Wasn't she happy and relieved to have Matt gone? Wasn't she glad to have seen the last of him, even if only for a week? She pulled the key out of her bag and turned it in the lock. Could it be that she found some sort of perverse pleasure in his company? Alison opened her front door and stepped into the darkened hallway, oblivious to Samson's welcoming cries and the soft feel of his body as he wound in and out around her legs.

She stared into the darkness with widened eyes. The truth was that Matt's presence had been an intoxicating stimulant that set her pulses racing and her heart beating with excitement. For the first time in her life, her job, her friends, and the events of Fairfax weren't quite enough. Some part of her wanted more, and this desire was greater than anything Alison had ever experienced. Matt's departure had left a void in her life, and the worst part of it, Alison realized with despair, was that only he could fill it.

Chapter Six

After the pale winter sun of Fairfax, Alison found herself almost blinded by the glaring brightness of the blue Florida sky. She squinted as she stepped off the airplane onto the tarmac, but just as she started to open her purse she realized that she had left her sunglasses back home on the shelf by the kitchen sink.

Alison shaded her eyes with one hand and followed the other passengers into Key West's small airport terminal. After placing her suitcase on the floor beside her, she stood hesitantly for a moment until her eyes became used to the indoor lighting. She had expected that Matt would be there to meet her, and as the plane had descended over the island she had found that her mouth had grown dry and that a permanent lump had claimed her throat. But now it seemed that all her fears were in vain. One by one the other passengers were greeted by friends and relatives, and Alison shortly found herself alone in the tiny waiting room. A small part of her felt panicky, a larger part was outraged that Matt had abandoned her, but for the most part she was profoundly disappointed not to see his tall, lean form striding toward her with his pantherlike grace.

"Excuse me, but are you Miss Alison Ramsey?"

Alison turned around to find a young woman approaching her, petite and elfin, with a cap of dark brown curls and big dark eyes.

"Yes . . . yes, I am."

"Matt sent me to meet you. He was unexpectedly called out of town yesterday and won't be back until dinnertime today. So I'm the welcoming committee."

Alison couldn't help but smile at the other woman's bubbling charm. "It's nice to meet you, Miss . . . ?"

"Walker, but please call me Terry; we're not very formal around here. I'm Matt's secretary, girl Friday, and chief cook and bottle washer." When Terry Walker smiled she had deep dimples in her cheeks and Alison reluctantly had to concede that Matt's secretary was very attractive. An impish little voice inside her also suggested that perhaps Terry Walker played an even more intimate role in Matt's life than that of secretary, but Alison hurriedly squelched the thought.

She reached down to pick up her suitcase but Terry had already retrieved it. "Here, let me help you. I'll take this so you can get the rest of your baggage from the claims counter."

"I don't have any other baggage," Alison replied.

Terry looked at her curiously, then down at the tiny suitcase. "You didn't bring very much," she said tentatively.

Alison shouldered her purse. "I'm not planning on staying long; it's just a business trip."

The other woman started to say something, then seemed to think better of it. "Of course," she said politely and then smiled, "Then it's time to go to the hotel. You look as if you could use a change of clothing."

Alison looked down at her crumpled navy-blue wool suit and grimaced as she looked back at Terry, cool and fresh-looking in a red sundress. Alison had worn a turtleneck sweater under her jacket, and she felt she was stifling even in the air-conditioned terminal. "It's hard to imagine that it can be so warm when you've just flown out of a snowstorm."

Terry nodded in agreement. "We've had wonderful

weather for the past month, warm and sunny every day. I'm sure you'll enjoy it." Then she pointed down a long corridor. "This way to the parking lot."

The Hotel Amérique was as big and as impressive as Alison remembered. Terry preceded her into the burgundy-and-gold lobby, took a key from the desk clerk, and led her to the elevators. As they got inside and headed upward, Terry began to explain how Matt ran his countrywide operations from the hotel. "Our main office is on the first floor—that's where the clerical staff and the architects work. The executive office is in the penthouse—you'll see how nice it is."

Alison murmured in agreement. She had no intention of letting Terry Walker know that she already had a more intimate knowledge of Matt's penthouse than was necessary.

Terry was chattering on. "Matt recently had a pool and sundeck built on the hotel roof off the penthouse, so now we don't have to use the pool in the main courtyard, which is for the guests. We don't bother them, and they don't bother us."

The elevator door opened at the sixth floor and Alison followed Terry out into the quiet corridor. "Is my room on this floor?"

"Yes—the suite. Here we are."

Terry opened the door at the end of the hallway, numbered 620, and ushered Alison in. "I think you'll find everything you need," she said as Alison put her bag on the floor. "Matt ordered a desk, typewriter, extra paper, and pens to be put in here for you."

Alison looked around. The suite's main room was very elegantly decorated with a French Provincial theme in cool blues and greens, and beyond it she could see an equally luxurious bedroom. "It looks very nice."

"It's one of our best rooms," Terry said, then walked over to one corner of the room and slid open a wooden folding door. "It even has a small kitchenette for snacks. Matt stocked it for you." She opened the door to the miniature refrigerator. "Butter, cheese, bread, some cold cuts—even a bottle of white wine."

"Matt seems to have thought of everything," Alison said dryly. She wouldn't be at all surprised if she also found a diaphanous nightgown in the bedroom and a key to the penthouse in the newly arrived desk.

Terry didn't seem to notice the sarcasm in Alison's voice. "Matt is very thorough and he never forgets a thing, but he's not fussy, if you know what I mean. I love working for him," she concluded enthusiastically.

Alison refrained from commenting, but she was almost beginning to wonder if she and Terry Walker were actually talking about the same man. The Matt she knew would make a terrible boss—arrogant, demanding, and unpredictable. But maybe, the little inner voice reminded her, the attractive Miss Walker knew Matt from a somewhat different perspective. Oh, shut up! she thought irritably and sat down wearily on one of the blue upholstered chairs.

Terry looked at her with sympathy. "You really do look hot and tired," she said. "Did you bring a bathing suit?" Alison nodded. "Why don't you have a rest and then come up to the penthouse and I'll show you the pool. I don't think anyone will be using it in the middle of the afternoon—we usually get our swim in during lunch or after work. That way you'll have it all to yourself."

"I . . . I thought that I'd start working right away."

Terry frowned. "Well . . . Matt gave strict instructions that only he was to show you around. He didn't mean to be away, but we had a problem at one of our hotels in San Francisco."

"Oh . . ." Alison said in a defeated tone. She should have known that Matt wasn't going to leave her on her own.

"You'll feel better after a rest." There was true concern in Terry's voice, and Alison smiled into her worried face.

"You're right," she finally conceded. "I'll unpack, lie down for an hour or so, and then have a swim. I must admit that the pool sounds wonderful."

Terry's expression lightened. "Good; I'll see you later. Do you think you can find your way to the penthouse?"

Alison's lips twitched slightly, but her voice gave nothing away. "I'm sure I can—don't worry about me."

"Have a good rest." With a dimpled smile, Terry left, closing the door quietly after her.

Alison sighed and then began to unpack. Besides her bathing suit, she had brought only a minimum of clothing. The blue silk dress that she had purchased over a month ago for that disastrous night in Key West had been left behind, pushed far back into the closet of her bedroom in Fairfax. It held too many embarrassing memories for her and, she suspected, provocative ones for Matt.

Slipping out of her heavy suit was a definite relief, and a quick shower in the green-tiled bathroom made her feel almost human again. After she had dried herself off with a thick lime-green towel she looked yearningly at the wide, immaculately made bed. Terry's suggestion of a short rest was seductive. Feeling vaguely wanton, although there was no one to see her, Alison slipped naked between the cool, crisp sheets. The room was dim, and the air conditioning hummed softly in the background. Occasionally a noise from the street below made its way to her room, but so muted that it did not disturb her. Alison dozed off, slipping deeper and deeper into a heavy afternoon sleep.

She dreamed of a pool made of green and white tiles and filled with sparkling turquoise water. She was standing beside it, still dressed in her navy wool suit and her black high heels. She was looking down into the center of the pool, where a photograph floated near the bottom. The odd thing was that the water didn't blur the face on the photograph but magnified it at least ten times. It was a photograph of Matt's face, and even through the depth of water the eyes on it seemed to penetrate right to her core.

There was a crowd of people around the pool, all of them strangers, and all of them yelling at her not to jump. But Alison knew that she had to have that photograph and that she was going to dive in, fully dressed. She took one step forward, then another . . . still another step until she stood right at the edge of the pool. The crowd grew silent, and she could hear the blue water lapping at the tiles. She held her eyes steady on the photograph, on the dark, gleaming eyes. . . .

"Wake up! Alison—wake up!"

The voice was loud in her ear, and rough hands were shaking her shoulder. Alison lifted her heavy eyelids and stared straight into Matt's worried face.

Matt! Alison shook her head slightly and came awake. He was standing beside her bed, handsome and tall in a light gray business suit.

"How did you . . . ?" Alison began to sit up and then suddenly realized that she was entirely naked. Coloring, she pulled the sheet up to her chin.

"Do you usually sleep so soundly?"

"What do you mean?" Alison brushed her blond hair off her face, not realizing that its tousled outline resembled a golden halo.

Matt, still frowning, sat down at the bottom of the bed. "Terry told me that you were here, but when I knocked there was no answer. I had the desk clerk phone your room, and still no answer. I was beginning to wonder if you'd had an accident, so I got the master key and let myself in. There you were, sleeping like a baby."

"I was . . . dreaming, I guess." Alison could still feel the mood of that dream, of that overwhelming desire to have the photograph no matter what it would take to get it. She looked away from Matt and down at her entwined fingers. She would never, in her wildest dreams, have imagined that, in reality, he would be seated at the bottom of her bed while she lay between the flimsy sheets without a stitch on.

"Only of me, I hope," he quipped, and Alison, glancing back up, could not help but notice that familiar glint in his eyes as he looked at her barely concealed body.

"Don't be such an egotist," she snapped back. "I have better things to dream about." Her fingers itched to grab the coverlet that was folded down by her ankles and drag it up over the sheet.

"Like what?" Matt leaned forward and Alison hastily grabbed a pillow and held it before her like a shield.

"Like . . . like dreaming of resorts that never get built."

Matt leaned back quickly, his lips twisted in anger. "Do you always have such a one-track mind?"

Alison clutched the pillow to her breasts, feeling helpless and vulnerable. "Isn't that why I came to Key West?"

Matt's eyes ran over her nude shoulders like an icy rain. "I had hoped that you would have a good time, too."

"I . . . maybe we just have different ideas of what constitutes a good time," Alison threw at him defiantly.

A muscle moved in his jaw. "Do you find relaxing so difficult?"

"I prefer to relax in my own home."

"Yes," Matt conceded dryly, "I noticed that."

Alison flushed at his allusion to their evening before the fire. "I would merely like to meet the architect and . . ."

"Forget the architect. You may be a workaholic, but I've just put in a solid twenty-four hours of negotiating with the staff at the Hotel Amérique in San Francisco and I'm going to spend the rest of the afternoon at the pool."

"But I would prefer . . ."

Matt's large hand grabbed the pillow that she held before her and his fingers brushed her skin. "If you don't promise to get your bathing suit on and join me at the pool in fifteen minutes, then I'm going to yank these sheets off you and dress you myself!"

Alison blanched at his threat. The tight line of Matt's mouth indicated that he would do exactly as he had said. "All right, I promise," she said hurriedly.

The tanned hand on the pillow loosened its grip and Matt straightened up. With a few long strides he was out of her bedroom and at the door of the suite. He turned just before heading into the corridor. "Remember, you have exactly fifteen minutes to get there."

For a few seconds Alison lay immobile in the bed, the sheet still pulled tight around her, the pillow still clasped in her arms. Some defense, she thought wryly, glancing down at the fine cotton material and the soft pillow. It was going to take armor of steel to ward off Matt Drake, not bed linens. And didn't Matt now have her exactly where he wanted her? Nude and in a bed that belonged to him? Alison sighed deeply and helplessly. Her relationship with Matt had all the earmarks of a losing battle. *Her* losing battle. Little by little, she had been maneuvered and enticed into positions that were favorable to Matt and threatening to herself.

She had to admit that Matt was winning. Two months ago she hadn't even known that he existed. Since then he had gotten her into his apartment, finagled a dinner invitation to her home, slept in her guest room, almost seduced her on her own living-room rug, and now . . . now she was smack-dab in the middle of enemy territory. Statistically speaking, the relationship was heading in only one direction, and Alison shivered slightly at the possibility of Matt's ultimate triumph.

But, she chided herself, statistics had nothing to do with it. Just because Matt was winning the minor skirmishes did not mean he would win the war. Alison still had faith in her own standards and her own willpower. They were stronger than steel, stronger than Matt's devastating arsenal of charm, looks, and sex appeal. She lifted her chin defiantly. She'd show Matt that, unlike the other women in his life, Alison Ramsey had no intention of surrendering.

Ten minutes later, dressed in a blue bikini, a white lace coverall, and sandals, and carrying a towel and a magazine, Alison made her way down the familiar quiet corridor and up the stairs to the penthouse door. When she turned the handle it swung open easily and without a sound. Alison took a step onto the thick white carpet and stood listening as she looked around. At the moment the apartment was silent and seemed to be deserted. To her right was the sunken living room with its brown leather furniture, and beyond that Matt's personal quarters. Then, from the hallway to her left, she heard the tapping of a typewriter and the insistent buzzing of a phone.

Alison walked past an unoccupied office and then peered into the next room. Terry Walker looked up from her typewriter just as Alison put her head in the doorway.

"There you are," she said with a smile. "I hear you had a good sleep."

"Yes, I feel much better."

Terry glanced at Alison's beach costume. "Ready for a swim, then? Matt said you'd be along." At Alison's nod, Terry stood up and then looked down at her desk, wrinkling her nose at the pile of papers on it. "I sure envy you a swim. Matt came back early with a week's worth of memos and reports."

"He said that he had staff problems." Alison was curious about how Matt ran his business.

"It was the manager. He'd been hired sight unseen, based on recommendations from another firm. He turned out to be a real lemon. I'll bet that's the last time Matt does that. He's always preferred to personally interview his managers, but this time he was in Europe and I guess this seemed to be the easiest way and . . ." Terry halted her rush of words and looked at Alison ruefully. "Sorry, this must be pretty boring to you. Come on, I'll show you the pool."

"Oh, don't apologize. I wasn't bored at all. I'm fascinated with Matt . . . er, with Matt's business," Alison stammered slightly. "I've never had any experience with a hotel-management firm before."

Terry didn't seem to notice Alison's slip of the tongue. "It *is* an interesting business," she agreed as she led Alison farther down the hallway. "Here we are." She pushed open a heavy outer door and Alison looked out onto the brilliantly sunlit roof of the Hotel Amérique, where a large oval pool had been constructed above the concrete on a frame of cedar planking.

"Matt just had this put in about three weeks ago," Terry explained, "so it's not finished yet—I think he's planning on a few cabanas and some more tables and chairs. Anyway, enjoy yourself. Matt will be along in a few minutes. One of the engineers had to see him."

Alison ventured onto the concrete surface and, wincing at the sun's bright rays, cursed her own stupidity at having left her sunglasses in Fairfax. The pool and its surrounding cedar deck lay exposed to the glare without either an awning or an umbrella to lend any welcoming shade. For a moment she hesitated, wondering whether she should dash down to the hotel's small shop in the lobby and buy some sunglasses. Then she realized that she was also missing suntan lotion and a hat, both of which required a real shopping expedition. She took another step forward; she'd just have to reconcile herself to burning to a crisp.

Before her, the roof of the hotel stretched out like a vast concrete runway, with guardrails on all sides and several protruding square cement boxes, which she guessed must house air-conditioning and heating units.

The pool had been built several yards from the penthouse door and there were half a dozen empty lounge chairs on the deck. As far as she could see, the place was deserted.

Alison climbed up to the deck and gazed down at the sparkling, shimmering water, debating whether to swim now or wait until Matt arrived. Considering the brevity of her bathing suit, she determined that being camouflaged by the water might be the safest strategy to follow when Matt was around. She'd wait until she heard him coming, then enter the water and stay there as long as possible. With that decided, she walked toward one of the lounge chairs and then stopped. Where was she going to sit without feeling like a steak that was being broiled to a turn? Suddenly, Alison had an inspiration. The pool and deck had to cast a shadow somewhere. She stepped over to the far edge of the deck and looked down at the shaded concrete. Of course, that was where she could go.

Alison folded a lounge chair, carried it down the steps, and walked around to the other side of the pool. When she had arranged the chair to her satisfaction, she slipped off her lace coverall and sandals, stretched out, and opened her magazine to a column about women in business. But as she began reading, she was distracted by the heat. Even in the shade the air was as hot as an oven, and Alison could feel small droplets of sweat forming on her upper lip. In two seconds she was going to throw strategy to the winds and immerse herself gratefully in the pool.

"We missed you last night, darling."

The voice came from the other side of the pool and it had the musical intonation characteristic of a Southern accent. Alison couldn't see the woman who had spoken, but she had seen the movie *Gone with the Wind* five times. That kind of lilting, seductive voice went with tiny waists, gauzy pastel dresses and wide hoopskirts, magnolia blossoms and the Civil War.

The male voice that answered was too low to allow Alison to hear the words, but the woman's voice chimed forth like the notes of a bell. "It was a fabulous party, and the band was divine. You really would have enjoyed it."

There was a jarring note of possession in that voice that contrasted strongly with its delicate, lovely accent. Alison found herself feeling a little bit sorry for whoever "darling" was. The woman sounded like a beauty, but she also sounded rapacious.

Alison squirmed in her lounge chair as she heard steps on the cedar deck about her head. She had no desire to be an eavesdropper. She was trying to decide how to extricate herself gracefully from the situation when the male voice responded once again.

"To tell the truth, Deanna, your friends' parties usually bore me."

The woman gave an uneasy laugh, as if this had not been the reply that she had expected, and Alison's estimation of "darling" climbed several notches. He didn't sound like a man possessed. He sounded very independent and sure of himself and . . . Alison sat forward in shock—she had suddenly recognized Matt's rich baritone.

"So, there you are." His voice was right above her head and Alison glanced up to see Matt looking down at her over the cedar fence that edged the deck. "Are you hiding?"

Alison scrambled to her feet, aware that, from his position, Matt had been able to look directly into the shadowed cleft between her partially exposed breasts. "No," she said hastily. "Just trying to stay in the shade. I . . . I forgot my sunglasses."

"Who are you talking to, darling?"

The woman had appeared beside Matt and was now also looking down at Alison with a cold and thorough perusal. Alison, in turn, noted that Matt's companion was very beautiful in an unexpected way. She was not at all the blond Southern beauty of Alison's imagination, but raven-haired and green-eyed, her classic features shaded by a wide-brimmed straw hat. From Alison's limited perspective, the other woman's silver bikini also revealed an exceptionally voluptuous figure.

"Deanna, this is Alison Ramsey of Fairfax, New York; Alison, this is Deanna O'Neill, a longtime friend of the family and the interior designer for our hotels."

The two women murmured greetings. Deanna's was so icy that, despite the heat, Alison felt a slight chill crawl up her spine. Deanna was obviously not pleased to meet her. From the small bit of conversation that she had overheard, Alison guessed that Deanna had a relationship with Matt that went beyond the bounds of either family friendship or business acquaintance. She felt an odd pang in her heart. While Alison knew, of course, that Matt had other women, somehow that fact had been easier to contemplate in the abstract. But now that reality was intruding in the seductive and glamorous form of Deanna O'Neill, Alison discovered that she liked it even less than she had expected.

Alison bit her lip and began to fold up her lounge chair. "I'll join you on the deck," she said.

"I'll help you with that chair," Matt replied, and before she could say that it wasn't necessary he had disappeared from sight.

Alison bent over and slipped her feet back into her sandals, all the while aware that Deanna was watching her and taking her measure as competition for the attentions of Matt Drake. She drew herself up to her full height and, throwing her blond hair off her forehead, looked Deanna straight in the eye. For a brief second their eyes locked and then the other woman turned away. Alison had a moment of triumph, which was immediately replaced by confusion. Since she had already determined that she wanted no part of a relationship with Matt, why did she care what his girl friend thought?

Alison's poise, already under pressure, was now challenged to the straining point by the sight of Matt coming toward her. Although the sight of his partially clad body was not new to her, Alison suddenly realized that she had never before actually had the opportunity to peruse him at such close quarters. As Matt strode toward her Alison wet her lips nervously and, not knowing exactly where to look, finally opted for her pink-varnished toes.

"Is there something wrong with your feet?" his sarcastic voice inquired. "Frankly, they look perfect to me."

Alison looked up slowly. "Uh . . . no. I was just thinking." She flushed at the way his eyes were making an impudent and slow tour of her own scantily covered form.

"A penny for your thoughts?" His hands were resting on his hips and everything about his muscular mahogany body spelled virility and confidence.

Alison's thoughts were far too embarrassing to share. She was fighting a growing and intense desire to touch Matt's broad chest, to follow the line of dark hair that curled over his flat stomach and ran to the waistband of his bathing suit. And that bathing suit! Black, silk, and so brief that it should be outlawed! With desperation, Alison grasped at her quickly receding sanity. "My thoughts are my own," she said with as much asperity as she could manage.

"Then you shouldn't have such expressive eyes," he rejoined with a flashing white grin, and Alison realized, with a sinking heart, that Matt knew only too well what her reaction to his physical presence had been.

"Aren't you coming in for a swim, Matt?" Deanna's sullen voice broke the deadlock between Alison and Matt, and he picked up the lounge chair while she hastily gathered up her coverall, towel, and magazine.

When Alison reached the deck she found Deanna emerging from the pool, every voluptuous curve emphasized by the clingy wet fabric of her bikini. To Alison's dismay, her initial impression of Deanna's beauty had been accurate. And the silver bikini, little more than three triangular pieces of cloth, left almost nothing to the imagination. It made Alison's turquoise suit seem almost sedate in comparison. Alison could understand why Matt had chosen to deepen his relationship with Deanna. Few men would be able to resist the allure of those rich and provocative curves.

Deanna settled down on a lounge chair and began to apply suntan oil to her long, beautiful legs. She turned as Matt came up on the deck behind Alison and unfolded the chair he was carrying. "Oh, darling, would you please do my back?"

Matt obediently came up behind her and took the bottle of lotion from her outstretched hand. Deanna nonchalantly unhooked the back strap of her bathing suit, her modesty only barely maintained by the forearm that she held before her breasts. With a seductive smile at Matt, she bent over so that he could apply the lotion to her naked back.

During this exchange Alison had been silently setting her belongings on a chair, and now she looked away from the couple beside her, unable to bear the sight of their intimacy or the way Matt's hand was caressing Deanna's tanned skin. Any action seemed better than just standing there with the sun beating down on her and her heart pounding in painful thuds. She quickly walked to the pool's edge and dove in, thankful for the cool obscurity of the water and the silent depths of the pool, where the sights and sounds of the scene on the deck could be obliterated.

Could it be that she was jealous? Alison pulled herself to the surface of the water, took a deep breath, and dove again. That was ridiculous, absurd, crazy —how could she be jealous over a man she didn't want? The trouble was that, for some reason, she didn't want Deanna O'Neill to have him, either. Alison couldn't understand herself or her emotions. They were contrary, perverse, and not very charitable—but then, there was something about being around Matt that seemed to bring out the worst in her.

She came up to the water's sparkling surface again to find Matt sitting on the pool's edge, watching her. "Enjoying the water?" he asked.

Alison shook the drops from her eyes. "It's very refreshing," she responded politely.

Suddenly he had slipped into the water near her. Alison looked up at the deck to see if Deanna was watching and then discovered that the other woman was gone. "Where's Deanna?"

"She had a phone call from one of our contractors in Houston; I have a feeling she won't be back."

"Oh . . . I see." It occurred to Alison that since the pool was so close to the office Matt could virtually run his business while getting a suntan. She smiled at him. "I'm surprised you don't have a phone out here. You seem to have thought of everything else."

Matt grimaced. "I decided that I wanted one place where I couldn't hear the phones ringing."

"It *would* be disruptive." Alison, shading her eyes, glanced at the intense blue sky above their heads and the deserted roof. Even the sounds from the street below were almost too faint to be heard.

"Yes," Matt agreed. "I didn't want to mix business with pleasure."

There was an unmistakable flash in his dark eyes and Alison quickly stepped backward, forgetting that the bottom dropped precipitously behind her. With a scream, she went under, her arms flailing. With a powerful thrust of his arms, Matt was beside her, pulling her up to the surface. Alison sputtered and blinked the water from her eyes. She was about to thank him and beat a hasty retreat to the deck when his arms slid around her and his mouth came down on hers. He pulled her slowly up against him until her feet no longer touched the bottom. Alison quivered as her body met his expanse of hard flesh, her breasts close to his chest, her legs against his. Of their own accord, her arms found their way around his neck and her hands ran over the muscular flesh of his bare shoulders.

There was, Alison discovered, something extremely sensual about making love in the water. The heat of the sun, the cool ripples of the water, the softness of Matt's lips, the feel of his warm wet skin, and the pressure of his hard thighs all combined to put her under a spell. She gloried in her own surge of desire and in the powerful reaction she had triggered in him. When his mouth left hers and his lips found the pulsing hollow of her throat she moaned.

He lifted his head and looked into her deep blue eyes with their spiky, wet lashes. "Now, *this* is what I call pleasure," he said, his voice husky. His curved lips moved toward her again and Alison placed one hand on his chest but made no effort to ward him off. Instead, she succumbed to an earlier desire and curved her fingers through the damp, springy hairs growing from his mahogany skin.

"Mr. Drake! Mr. Drake!" a voice called from the direction of the penthouse, and then a door slammed.

Matt groaned expressively and moved away, letting Alison down slowly. "And here comes business." He pulled himself out of the pool and was wrapping a towel around his shoulders as a young girl climbed up the stairs onto the deck.

Alison, her body still trembling and aching from the loss of Matt, stood stock-still in the water. The girl was, she estimated, no more than eighteen years old and very pretty, with her dark eyes and auburn hair parted in the middle and hanging down her back in luxuriant waves. Even from a distance Alison could see the look of admiration the girl bestowed on Matt's lean, bronzed form. The ache in her body was now augmented by a tremor in her heart. For a few seconds she had also

119

forgotten the attractive Terry Walker and the seductive Deanna O'Neill. It would seem that Matt liked to surround himself with beautiful women. In that case, Alison reflected with an odd catch in her throat, he must consider her nothing more than another notch in his already well notched belt.

"Mr. Drake, could you sign this for Miss Walker? It has to go out this afternoon." The girl was holding out a document and a pen.

Matt signed the papers and then turned as Alison pulled herself wearily out of the pool. "Melissa, I'd like you to meet Miss Ramsey. She's going to help us with the planning of the Fairfax Hotel."

"Hi, Miss Ramsey," the younger girl gushed at her as Alison wrapped a towel around her dripping body.

"It's nice to meet you, Melissa." Alison bestowed a warm smile on the younger girl, but the effort to be pleasant was difficult. The girl had eyes only for Matt, and even Alison had to admit that, despite her youth, Melissa had a lot to offer. The little blue cotton dress she was wearing revealed a quickly maturing womanly form and lovely legs.

"Oh, Mr. Drake, Miss Walker would like to see you as soon as possible. The manager of the Chicago hotel phoned about fifteen minutes ago and he was worried about . . ."

Matt held up a hand. "Spare me the details for a few minutes, Melissa. I'll learn about them all too soon. Go ahead and tell Terry that I'm coming. Here, take the papers."

When Melissa had walked down the steps and entered the penthouse, Matt turned to Alison and began to pull her back into his arms. "I'm sorry about the interruption," he murmured.

Alison jerked away. "Well, I'm not!"

Matt's lips quirked. "That's odd; I had the feeling that the pleasure was mutual."

Alison pulled the lace coverall over her head. Matt's

120

eyes had rested once too often on her cleavage and slim hips. "I . . . it's the heat. I'm a bit . . . dizzy."

Matt tossed his towel over one broad shoulder and gave her a dashing smile. "It's always nice to know that my lovemaking has some effect."

Alison looked quickly down at the sandals she was slipping onto her bare feet. If only Matt weren't so handsome! "I told you—I was dizzy from the sun," she murmured stubbornly.

With one stride Matt was in front of her and his hand lifted her chin, forcing her to look at him. "Then, sweetheart," he said, giving her a chaste kiss on her forehead, "I hope you're always in the sun."

He was down the steps before Alison could think of a suitable retort and had reached the door of the penthouse when he turned around. "I'll see you for dinner at the Pavillon. Six-thirty sharp."

Alison began to refuse the dinner invitation but he was already gone. She sat down on a chair and, shading her eyes with her hands, looked at the shimmering, glistening water as if it could solve her dilemma. Matt had just won another battle. The shameful truth was that Matt's desire for her was equaled by her desire for him. Her body had not cared that he probably had more girl friends than he needed. Only her mind flinched at the thought. And it was becoming more and more evident that her mind had absolutely no control over her body.

Alison dreaded dinner that evening and wondered if she could plead a headache. Then she recalled how Matt had entered her room when she had been sleeping. If she complained of a headache, no doubt he would ply her with aspirin and insist that she have something to eat anyway. Alison took a deep breath and squared her shoulders. Maybe she should use a different tactic. Maybe the best way to overcome her enemy was to study his strategy. The more she knew about Matt, the more weapons she would have to fend him off. Even now the thought of Terry Walker, Melissa, and Deanna O'Neill was enough to stiffen her spine. One kiss in the pool, she decided, meant nothing at all. As far as she was concerned, the war was far from over.

Chapter Seven

Alison knocked on the door of the conference room in the office wing of the penthouse, but when there was no answer she pushed it open and entered. The room was just as she remembered it: walls covered with blueprints and maps and a long central table surrounded by leather chairs. Alison surveyed the empty room, switched on the lights, and chose a chair near the middle of the table. She had known that she would be a little early for the morning meeting, but she was thankful for some extra time to be alone and to sort out her thoughts.

Dinner with Matt the night before had not been what she had expected. The food and ambiance had been as luxurious as before, but the ardent and teasing lover of the afternoon had turned into a cordial but aloof businessman. Alison thought she could attribute some of Matt's subdued manner to his evident exhaustion. The trip to San Francisco and the hours of negotiations had obviously sapped even Matt's extraordinarily alert and dynamic personality.

But his aloofness had confused her. Although their conversation had never lagged—they had discussed every subject from modern art to gourmet cooking—his attitude toward her had been casual. And Alison had discovered, to her chagrin, that she was more hurt by his indifference than relieved.

They had parted early in the evening and Alison had entered her room in a state of bewilderment. Didn't she want Matt to treat her as a casual acquaintance rather than as a potential lover? Wasn't that the reason she resisted his lovemaking? Yet, when her actions seemed to have gained the desired result, all she felt was let down and disappointed.

Tossing and turning for most of the night, she had only fallen into a deep sleep in the small hours of the morning. The hotel's wake-up service had called her promptly at 7:30, as she had requested, so that she would be prepared for the nine o'clock meeting, but she had dozed off for another hour despite all intentions to be up early. When she had finally awakened and looked at her wristwatch she had been galvanized into immediate action.

Now, as she smoothed down the skirt of her gray linen suit and straightened the bow at the neck of her white silk blouse, she felt her stomach grumble in protest. She had skipped breakfast in her haste to be ready, and now she wondered how she was going to make it through to lunch. She nervously rearranged the pack of paper before her and pulled a pen and a pencil from her purse. Matt had organized this conference specifically for her, and, famished or not, she had to give the appearance of alertness, intelligence, and concentration.

"Good morning, madam."

The door had opened behind her and a waiter was wheeling in a tray with a coffeepot and cups. Following behind him was a short, wiry, gray-haired man in his mid-fifties, dressed in a dark business suit and carrying a large portfolio. He smiled as he saw Alison and stretched out his hand.

"You must be Miss Ramsey. I'm John Brennan, an architect with Matt's firm."

Alison stood up and shook his hand. She knew that Matt's chief architect was going to give a presentation, but she had expected someone far more formidable than this friendly man who was now sitting opposite her.

The waiter was pouring the coffee and put a cup beside Alison. Its delicious aroma wafted to her nostrils and her stomach protested again. Alison held the cup between her hands and took a sip, hoping that the coffee would stave off famine for the next few hours.

"Have you been in Key West before?" John Brennan accepted a cup of coffee from the hovering waiter and stirred in a teaspoonful of sugar.

"Yes, once." It seemed that Matt had told no one about her previous trip to Key West or their evening in the Pavillon.

"Then you've probably seen all the tourist attractions?" John Brennan looked at her inquiringly, but Alison didn't disabuse him of the notion, although she had been so tired during her week's stay that she had done virtually nothing but lounge by the pool. "You should get Matt to take you out diving on the coral reef," he continued. "It's quite an experience."

Alison was just about to say that it sounded like more of an experience than she could handle when the door opened again and three people entered. There was a stocky blond man of middle height whom Alison had never seen before, then Matt, tall, tanned, and handsome in a light blue suit, and Deanna O'Neill. The last two had been laughing together at some joke as they walked through the door and Deanna had placed a possessive hand on Matt's arm. Alison felt her back stiffen. She'd had enough of Matt and Deanna's intimacies at the pool and now hoped fervently that she wouldn't be subjected to any more.

Matt made the introductions. "I see that you've met John, Alison. He's our chief architect, and this is David Shaw," he said, bending his dark head in the stocky man's direction. "He's our chief engineer. And of course you've already made Deanna's acquaintance."

The two women smiled frostily at each other. Deanna, Alison noted, had not let business interfere with her flamboyant fashion sense. She was wearing a flaming scarlet silk dress with a scoop neckline and a straight skirt that emphasized every full curve. She made Alison feel positively dowdy in her tailored gray suit. Deanna's raven tresses had been waved and swept into a sophisticated hairstyle and Alison unconsciously smoothed her own ash-blond hair in its simple bell shape. Her hairdresser in Fairfax was always trying to convince her to experiment with her thick straight hair, but Alison had always adamantly refused. Now she was regretting her conservatism.

Matt had opened the meeting. "As you all know, Miss Ramsey is here to report on the plans for the Fairfax hotel–resort complex to the town residents. Each of you has been called in to this conference to present a brief summary to Miss Ramsey of your particular area of concern. John, I think we'll begin with you."

John Brennan's large portfolio contained dozens of blueprints of the proposed buildings. He hung each one on the easel that stood by the conference table and offered a short but detailed explanation. While the others watched him attentively, Alison scribbled madly on the paper before her. As one sketch followed another she had to concede to a feeling of admiration. The proposed resort was tasteful, would blend in with the local terrain, and would not detract from the scenery. The interior rooms, including a commons area with a large stone fireplace, a dining area almost completely enclosed by glass windows, and three wings of private accommodations, were well organized and luxurious.

"Any questions, Alison?"

She looked up to see Matt's eyes on her and shook her head. The aloof businessman of the night before was very much in evidence this morning. Despite the fact that he had called her by her first name, Matt was treating her with cool politeness and reserve. She could barely equate him with the passionate lover of that night in Fairfax, or the flirtatious playboy who had kissed her in the pool just the day before.

David Shaw was next. His domain was the nuts-and-bolts construction of the buildings and the adjoining pool and ski hill. Alison exclaimed in surprise when she heard about the latter, and Matt stopped David in midsentence. "Is something bothering you, Alison?"

"Where will the ski hill be situated?" Alison was genuinely perplexed. The Derrick farm was almost completely flat.

David Shaw placed a large map of the farm and the surrounding area on the easel. "The stream that runs behind the farm flows downhill into the adjoining property. The slope created by the stream will provide an adequate angle for a small ski hill."

"But," Alison said with a frown, "doesn't a ski tow have to be constructed at the bottom of the hill?" The Merriams owned the property adjoining the farm's western boundary, and she was positive that a barn stood by the very stream that David Shaw was indicating.

"Well . . . of course." He had a confused expression and looked at Matt for help.

"We've taken an option on the property that adjoins the Derrick farm," Matt said smoothly, looking directly at Alison through hooded eyes. "Does that answer your question?"

Alison nodded slowly and then looked down at her pad, allowing her long eyelashes to fan across her cheeks and hide the stunned look in her eyes. Matt's response had more than adequately answered her question. It had proved to her, beyond the shadow of a doubt, that the resort threatened more than a takeover of the Derrick farm. Matt's ambitions were not limited to one property. With an option on another, he could expand to his heart's content. Alison clenched her teeth and jotted a note on her pad. She felt angry, frustrated, helpless, and vulnerable. How many other unpleasant revelations was Matt going to spring on her this morning?

David Shaw was discussing access roads and traffic when the mention of High Ridge Road caught Alison's attention. Matt's firm, she learned, would be suggesting to hotel guests that they bypass downtown Fairfax and use one of the country roads that ran through the surrounding farmlands. As she followed the route that David Shaw was pointing out, Alison sat forward. "I wonder . . ." she began.

He stopped and everyone at the table turned to look at her.

"Yes, I'm positive. That route is fine until you hit the intersection with High Ridge Road." They all looked back at the map and David Shaw held his pointer to the spot Alison had mentioned. "All our schools are located about a mile from High Ridge Road—halfway to Fairfax. In the summer, the schools are used as day camps, so there are buses and children at that intersection virtually all year long."

David Shaw rubbed his chin. "That could be dangerous."

"Are there any other alternatives, Dave?" Matt asked crisply.

"Well, we could move traffic over here onto Meadow Creek Road, but it's in pretty bad condition."

Matt turned to Alison. "Does the town have any plans for improvement?"

Alison shook her head emphatically and her blond hair swung from side to side. "Meadow Creek Road has so little traffic that the road committee decided to use its tax money elsewhere."

"Dave, have you looked into the municipal regulations or talked to anyone about road improvements?"

"No, we didn't think it would be a problem," Dave

said a bit reluctantly, "so I don't have any answers right now."

Matt was cool and decisive. "Make that your number-one priority. I'd like to have information on it by tomorrow."

David Shaw nodded and then concluded his summary with a brief closing statement.

"Deanna?" Matt turned toward the woman who was sitting close beside him.

After the concise and factual summaries of the architect and engineer, Deanna's report was a plunge into the world of sensations, both visual and tactile. She showed them sketch after sketch of color-coordinated rooms and passed around swatches of material in what seemed to be every color, design, and fabric.

Alison saw and handled samples of chenille, velvet, damask, silk, terry cloth, percale, broadcloth, brocade, and linen. Chips of linoleum and ceramic tile made their way around the table. Rectangular pieces of carpet, carved, tufted, woven, and plain, were distributed and then tossed back into a voluminous bag. She saw catalogs of lamps, bathroom fixtures, beds, chairs, desks, tables, dressers and lawn furniture. By the time Deanna was through with her presentation, Alison's head was spinning.

"Any questions?"

"No," she said, "it all seems very nice." The other woman smiled smugly, to Alison's annoyance. She hated to compliment the already arrogant Deanna, but, in all honesty, the other woman had done a superlative job. Alison had been especially impressed with the main rooms. The dining area was to have chairs of striped velvet in a shantung rose and slate blue, matching blue tablecloths, and contrasting ivory drapes. The commons room would be less formal but no less elegant, with deep couches of russet corduroy and chestnut leather standing on multicolored and patterned oriental rugs. Deanna had also shown a startling variety of color schemes for the guest apartments, ranging from whimsical daisy yellows and apple greens to luxurious ivories, taupes, and grays.

"Fine, thanks, Deanna." The other woman, still cool and unruffled after an information-packed thirty-minute demonstration, began to gather her samples together. "That will be all, then, I believe," Matt went on, "and I thank you for coming. I'm sure Miss Ramsey is most appreciative of your time and effort"—Alison smiled—"and if she has any further questions I'll have her go directly to each of you."

There was a rustle as they all stood up and papers and briefcases were gathered and closed. David Shaw and John Brennan filed out quickly, but Deanna lingered. "I'll be waiting for you, Matt," she said, standing in the doorway to the conference room.

Matt gave her a cursory glance as he closed his portfolio. "I'll be in my office."

Deanna smiled and then disappeared, leaving Matt and Alison alone.

"I don't know how to thank you," Alison began, but Matt waved aside her words.

"No problem, all part of the day's work." He strode toward the door and then turned to face Alison, who was still standing behind her chair. His eyes made a quick but thorough study of her smooth blond hair, soft silk blouse, and trim gray suit, but his voice was noncommittal. "I have a meeting scheduled through lunch, but I want to see you at three. Will that be convenient?"

Alison looked at him warily. "Yes. What do you want to see me about?"

"Further plans," he said abruptly and left the room.

Alison sighed and her stomach growled. She had quite forgotten about the breakfast she had missed and had not noticed how the morning had disappeared. She stretched slightly and walked out into the hallway. Matt was nowhere in sight and the corridor was quiet. She decided on a quick lunch at a nearby coffee shop, a visit to a drugstore to buy sun cream and the sunglasses she so sorely needed, and then several hours working in her room. She had promised to give George a telephone report the following morning, and her initial impressions of the resort would have to be in some kind of organized form before then.

Alison lifted her head and wearily rubbed the aching muscles at the back of her neck. Her desk was cluttered with sheet upon sheet of scribbled-on paper holding all her impressions of the resort gathered during the conference that morning. On the whole, her opinion was favorable, and that bothered her a great deal. Because she was honest, she was going to have to give the resort a positive report, but it was going to be galling. She still opposed the resort on principle, and this was enforced by the knowledge that Matt's firm might gobble up surrounding property if the hotel were a success. She planned to include that in the report as well.

Alison wound a blank sheet of paper into the typewriter, intending to transpose her scribbled notes into a more coherent form, and then looked at her wristwatch. Two-thirty—not enough time to get anything accomplished before her meeting with Matt. Alison stood up and walked over to her window, which overlooked the busy street below. The sun was shining from a brilliant and cloudless turquoise sky and the tourists were out in force, enjoying the balmy Southern sun and the island's assortment of boutiques and shops. If Matt didn't keep her too long, she might get a chance to have a walk and stretch her stiff legs.

A quick peek in the mirror established that she looked rumpled from her hours at the desk. She brushed her white-blond hair until it shone and applied a pale pink lipstick to her lips. Yesterday's exposure to the sun had painted a faint glow on her cheeks that highlighted the blue-green of her eyes and eliminated the need for makeup. She had changed from her suit into a more comfortable sundress, a white cotton with tiny flowers of jonquil yellow, mint green, and navy blue. It had a low, square neckline with narrow shoulder straps and a snug bodice that tapered to a belted waistline and a slightly flared skirt. She smoothed the wrinkles out of the skirt and slipped on high-heeled white sandals. Another appraisal in the mirror indicated that, while she might not be as glamorous as Deanna O'Neill, she was still tall, slender, and attractive.

When Alison entered Matt's office he stood up and his eyes took on that familiar gleam. She had the feeling that the cool businessman of last night and this morning had been replaced by the Matt she knew all too well. Alison stiffened slightly as his gaze ran over her and prepared herself for the forthcoming skirmish.

"Sit down, Alison, while I just get these papers organized."

She sat in the leather chair before his desk and looked around his office. It was neat and orderly, with folders stacked in piles, several filing cabinets, and shelf upon shelf of books.

The intercom buzzed gently and Matt, with a grimace of annoyance, pressed one of the buttons. Terry Walker's voice came through the speaker. "Sorry to bother you, Matt, but that phone call from Alaska has finally come in and I didn't think you'd want to miss it."

Matt spoke into the intercom. "Okay, I'll take it." He looked at Alison. "Sorry about this," he said, and then pressed a button on his telephone and picked up the receiver. "Matt Drake here . . . Yes, I did get your message about the steel shipment . . ."

Alison's attention wandered and she stood up and walked around Matt's office. One shelf held a row of photographs and she looked at these with curiosity. One gilt-framed picture was of a gray-haired man bearing a strong resemblance to Matt, and Alison surmised that this was his father. There was a wedding photo of a young couple, and beside that one of a cute girl baby, with fat roly-poly legs and a toothless grin. His sister and niece? Alison's attention was finally centered on the large photograph of an older woman, regal and haughty, her graying hair wound into a coronet of braids. Was this Matt's mother?

"Elizabeth Schwarzenville."

Alison turned to find Matt standing behind her. He had the most uncanny way of silently sneaking up on a person. "I beg your pardon?"

"Elizabeth Schwarzenville," Matt repeated. "After my mother died, she brought up my sister, Jane"—he pointed to the smiling bride—"and myself."

"Oh—I'm sorry. I didn't realize . . . I mean, I thought when you said your father had retired that your mother was with him."

"My father is retired—I think he's sunning himself on the Riviera right now. But my mother died when I was five. Elizabeth was her sister; she's from Switzerland."

"Your father never remarried?"

Matt looked grim and Alison could see the muscles moving in his lean, tanned jaw. "My father should never have married in the first place. I don't remember much about it, but I know that he made life miserable for my mother."

There was something in his voice that gave Alison an inkling of what Matt must have been like as a small boy, caught between the makers of a loveless marriage. "That must have been hard on you and your sister," she said sympathetically.

Matt's dark eyes held a bitter look. "My father was so caught up in his business that he didn't even remember that his family existed most of the time. I'm still surprised that he actually retired. But he's the

133

reason I never . . ." Shutters dropped over his dark eyes and he shrugged his wide shoulders. "What's past is past. I believe in living for the present."

Alison, tactfully realizing that Matt had no wish to delve into painful memories, teased him gently. "That's a pretty hedonistic viewpoint—to live only for the pleasures of the moment."

A grin eased the stark, chiseled lines of his face. "That's my idea of heaven—wine, women, and song." His glance ran over her body and Alison felt as if she were being stripped right down to her bare skin.

She backed away and sat primly in the leather chair. "You had some business to discuss with me?"

Matt shoved both hands into his pants pockets and his blue jacket swung open to reveal a crisp white shirt that was molded to his wide chest and flat stomach. "Actually, I've had enough of business today. I want you to come for a ride with me."

"A ride? Where?"

"When we had that . . . er, unusual"—and he grinned slightly as Alison winced—"evening at the Pavillon, you mentioned that you had never been on a tour of the island. I'm appointing myself as official tour guide."

Alison spoke hurriedly. "That's . . . that's very nice of you, but I still have to type up my notes from this morning's meeting and . . ."

Matt took his hands from his pockets and walked up to her chair. Suddenly dizzy, Alison looked away from his tall, dominating form. "Still afraid of me?" he murmured wickedly.

"Of course not," she bristled and looked up defiantly.

Thick dark eyelashes did not conceal the glints in his eyes. "I don't usually make passes in broad daylight—your virtue will remain intact."

Alison was not about to remind him about the previous day's kiss. That had certainly occurred in broad daylight, and it had threatened the very virtue he was talking about. "I don't know . . ." she said hesitantly.

To her surprise, he grabbed her hand and pulled her to a standing position. "Come on, all work and no play makes Alison a dull girl."

Alison knew when she was defeated. Matt was persuasive and persistent and, as usual, would not take no for an answer. Besides, Alison recalled her desire to get out of the hotel and onto Key West's bustling streets. She didn't really intend to type those notes until the evening anyway. "All right," she yielded with a deep sigh.

"You don't have to make it sound like such torture. Just think of the dozens of fair damsels who would give their right arms to have me as their . . . tour guide."

Alison didn't miss his teasing emphasis on the last two words. Tour guide, indeed! Alison had a very good idea of what kind of tour Matt was referring to, but she wouldn't give him the satisfaction of even a knowing smile. The trouble was that Alison knew there was more truth to his assertion than she liked to admit. There were plenty of women—Deanna and Melissa, to name just two—who were eager for Matt's undivided attention. She suddenly became aware that her hand was still engulfed in his warm one. She snatched it away from him and picked up her purse. "When do we go?" she asked, her voice flat.

"I'll meet you in ten minutes in front of the hotel." His phone buzzed insistently and Matt gestured helplessly. "Better make that fifteen."

Alison was standing under the hotel's gilt portico exactly fifteen minutes later, staring at the passing crowd but not really seeing it. She was, she discovered, totally mystified by Matt's rapid changes of mood. Since she had arrived in Key West he had been first ardent, then cold and reserved, then warm and teasing. She couldn't predict what he would do next, and his swift alterations of personality had her on tenterhooks. If only she knew precisely how Matt would act then she would know precisely how to respond. But every change caught her unprepared and confused. Perhaps, Alison thought wryly, this was Matt's strategy against her resistance. Keep the enemy guessing and he was virtually guaranteed a victory.

Alison's thoughts were interrupted as a sleek maroon sports car with its top down pulled up in front of the hotel with Matt at the wheel. She slipped into the seat next to him, hastily pulling down her skirt, which had risen to reveal a long expanse of tanned leg. Matt, needless to say, had not missed one inch. As she closed her door, Alison bet that he drove the low-slung sports car for just that reason—it would make any woman's entry somewhat less than elegant.

"Ready?"

At Alison's nod the car sprang forward with a powerful surge and Matt pulled it smoothly into traffic. With the top down, Alison could feel the wind tug at her hair as if it had fingers. She pulled the sunglasses off the top of her head and onto her nose and for a moment attempted to shield her hair with one hand.

"Do you want the top up?" Matt's eyes were on the traffic but he was aware of every movement that she made.

"No." Alison threw her head back and allowed the wind to play havoc with her hair. It gave her a glorious, unfettered feeling, as if she were totally carefree and not burdened with a job and civic responsibilities, as if she and Matt were alone in some different world.

Alison studied him from behind her concealing dark glasses. Neither sun nor wind seemed to bother him. He wore no sunglasses and his thick dark hair was sleeked back by the rushing air. He had changed from his suit into a cream knit sports shirt and matching slacks. The short sleeves revealed thick biceps the color of mahogany and muscular forearms sprinkled with fine dark hair. He drove skillfully and his hands looked masterful and competent on the racing-style wheel. He didn't seem inclined to talk as he drove and Alison finally allowed herself to be absorbed by the passing scenery.

They were leaving the island's shopping district and heading into a maze of streets with houses that looked as if they had been built at the turn of the century. Many of them were charming, with wide spacious porches and freshly painted walls and trim. Their gardens bloomed with the colors of the rainbow: the pale yellow blossoms of acacia, the reddish-purple bougainvillea, and many others that Alison did not recognize. Palm trees, thick with coconuts, were everywhere.

Matt slowed down and pointed out various landmarks. "The Audubon House," he said, waving at a large, gracious white mansion with green foliage in front, "where John James Audubon painted the Florida birds."

There were other famous houses. Ernest Hemingway, America's Nobel Prize–winning novelist, had lived on Key West for ten years, and President Harry Truman had established a residence called the Little White House.

Alison was intrigued by the older houses and noticed that many had cables running from their roofs to the ground. In answer to her question, Matt had a terse answer: "Hurricanes."

"Hurricanes?"

"You're just an ignorant Northerner," he teased. "Since the Keys are really only part of a coral reef above the water, there's no real soil to build on. None of our houses have foundations. If they weren't cabled to the ground, they'd fly away in the hurricane season."

Alison also noticed that many houses had widow's

walks, small wooden platforms with guardrails that sat on the roofs, built to allow a sailor's wife to overlook the ocean to see if her husband's ship was returning.

"Most of the island's history is bound up with the ocean," Matt explained. "Not all of it is too savory, I'm afraid."

"What do you mean?"

"The island's first big industry was salvaging wrecked ships. Spanish galleons and other cargo ships made their way to the Atlantic but plenty of them couldn't navigate through the reefs. When they foundered and broke, the early islanders would make money salvaging the cargo and saving the crew."

"That doesn't sound so unsavory to me."

Matt turned onto the road that ran around the end of the island, circling the miles of beach and ocean. "It was—when the islanders neglected to warn the ships or help them, so that they ended up totally demolished. Then, of course, there were the pirates."

"Now, *that* sounds romantic."

Matt grinned at her. "Even when legend has it that the trees on the island were decorated with the bodies of pirates after they were hanged?"

Alison wrinkled her nose. "Ugh."

"You know what the name Key West means?" Alison shook her head. "It's an anglicized version of *Cayo Hueso*—Spanish for Bone Island. When the first Spanish sailors came, the island was strewn with human bones, probably those of early Indians."

"I didn't know Key West had such a bloody history."

"Well, I like to think that the Drake family has a few swashbucklers in its past." He grinned at her again and Alison's mind made an imaginative leap. Matt himself would have been the perfect pirate. Pantaloons, a bared tanned chest, an eye patch, and a sharp knife clenched between his gleaming white teeth suited his personality far better than a tailored business suit.

Alison smiled to herself but asked curiously, "Is your family from Key West?"

"Of course. Otherwise I'd be totally crazy to have my corporate headquarters in the southeasternmost tip of the United States. It would be a lot more logical if I had offices in New York or Los Angeles—even Miami—but I prefer to be here."

Alison looked at him in surprise. Matt's disregard for her own feelings for Fairfax had led her to believe that he lacked all softer feelings. It had never occurred to her that Matt could feel affection for the area he grew up in. It seemed to make him more vulnerable, not at all the man that she thought she knew. She wondered how many other aspects of Matt's personality were hidden from her and she recalled his bitterness about his father. Alison glanced at his chiseled profile, but it told her nothing. Matt, she suspected, was the kind of man who kept a tight lid on his innermost feelings.

They were stopped at a red light. When it turned green Matt drove for only a few feet and then pulled into a parking lot beside a restaurant. "Now for a real treat," he announced.

Alison was wary. "What sort of treat?"

"It's time for dinner and I don't think you can be allowed to stay in Key West without trying its specialty."

He would say nothing more and Alison followed helplessly into the restaurant, whose dimly lit interior was cool and refreshing after the bright sun. The place was called Neptune's Cave and was decorated in the style of an old ship, complete with portholes, oars, wheels, and nets on its planked wooden walls.

Alison made a quick retreat to the washroom and performed a repair job on her windblown hair. The sun and breeze, she noted, had turned the faint blush on her cheeks into a deeper shade of pink. It was not unattractive, but, unfortunately, her nose promised to turn the same color. Alison applied a light dusting of powder and then shrugged. Matt should surely be used to sunburns by now.

When she returned to their table Alison discovered that Matt had already ordered their dinner, but despite all her efforts she could not get him to reveal what she was going to eat.

"I want you to taste it first."

"It must be something horrible," she finally concluded, "like—oh, I don't know—chocolate-covered ants. When I was a kid, that was the worst thing I could think of."

"You'll see" was his mysterious reply.

"Matt! Fancy seeing you here!"

A tall, elegant woman was coming toward the table. She was not young, perhaps in her late forties, Alison estimated, but her age did nothing to detract from her looks. She had sleek platinum hair pulled back into a smooth chignon, a strand of luminous pink pearls around her neck, and a mauve silk and chiffon dress whose every line proclaimed its couturier designing.

Matt rose, kissed the older woman lightly on the cheek, and introduced her to Alison. Her name was Danielle Chenier, and she was the owner of La Ronde, one of the island's most exclusive dress shops. Alison had perfect recall about La Ronde. On the day she had shopped for her blue dress she had made the mistake of stopping there. The boutique's dresses had been glamorous and elegant, but their prices had matched them in magnificence, and Alison had beaten a hasty retreat to a shop slightly more in sympathy with her bank balance. Danielle Chenier, she now guessed, would have no such bourgeois qualms.

Danielle was gracious in her welcome to Alison, but she was interested only in Matt. "Where have you been?" she asked him. "I called you last week *and* the week before."

Alison listened to their animated conversation with

only half an ear. She was far more interested in their body language. Matt, who had remained standing, was smiling down at the older woman as she spoke and she in turn was emphasizing a point by placing her hand on his wrist in a possessive motion. It suggested to Alison that perhaps at one time they had been lovers.

How can you think such things? she rebuked herself, but then gave a mental shrug. What else was she to think? They obviously knew each other very well, and Alison was certainly becoming accustomed to having Matt's women spring up everywhere. There was Deanna, his present-day mistress; Melissa, a potential one; and now Danielle Chenier, an intimate from an earlier period in Matt's life. And, of course, there was Terry Walker, whose status remained ambiguous. Alison looked away from the chatting couple and down at the napkin she was wringing in her hand. There were times, she decided furiously, when she would like to wring Matt's neck.

"Do you want to join us?" Matt made a welcoming gesture, but to Alison's relief the older woman shook her head.

"Sorry, but I have to get back to the shop. We had a big shipment from Paris today and I want to have it on the racks tomorrow, even if it means working all night. I'll get in touch with you soon." She made her goodbyes and walked back to her table, leaving a musky trace of perfume behind.

Danielle's departure coincided with the arrival of their waiter. He placed steaming bowls of soup before them and set a large basket of rolls and crackers on the side. As he walked away Alison stared at the creamy golden liquid, thick with chunks of meat. "Okay," she said warily, "what is it?"

"Take a taste." Matt grinned at her and then dipped his own spoon into the soup.

Alison cautiously lifted the steaming liquid to her mouth and sipped at it. It wasn't terrible; in fact, it was quite good. It tasted like . . . like . . . Alison couldn't quite put her finger on it. "All right," she said, "I've tasted it—now, what is it?"

"Conch soup."

"What?" He had pronounced the word as if it were spelled c-o-n-k.

"Conch soup—it's made from the animals that live inside the conch shells."

Alison put her spoon down abruptly. "You mean those huge pink and white shells collected from the ocean?"

"Yes, good, isn't it?"

Alison stared at the golden broth. "I'm not sure," she said a bit shakily.

"I thought you had a sense of adventure," Matt said with one dark eyebrow raised in a mocking arch. He took a deep spoonful of the soup and then reached for a roll.

Alison took another hesitant sip. "I think," she said, as her stomach took a definite nose dive, "that my sense of adventure has deserted me."

Matt glanced at her face and took pity on her. "I've also ordered us steak," he said and then grinned at her obvious sigh of relief. "Here, have a roll."

The success of the rest of their dinner gave Alison the courage to insist upon paying her portion of the bill in spite of Matt's protests.

"I don't want to owe you anything," she explained stubbornly.

Matt's lips quirked. "I see—not like last time?"

Alison flushed, remembering the way Matt had collected his debt. "Not like last time," she agreed with determination. To her satisfaction, Matt demurred gracefully.

As they drove back to the Hotel Amérique, Alison asked Matt about his trip to San Francisco. She was curious to know how he resolved his personnel problems, feeling that if she could have a glimpse of how he ran his business she might understand him better.

The ensuing conversation engrossed them right up until Matt delivered Alison to her hotel room. ". . . Although the manager hadn't lived up to his end of the contract I still gave him the severance pay," Matt was saying as they approached Room 620. "I believe in honoring my agreements to my employees even when they don't deserve it."

They halted before the door as Alison fumbled in her purse for the key. When she finally pulled it out she looked up to find Matt standing dangerously close.

"Alison . . ." he began, and deep fires seemed to flare in his eyes.

She stiffened. "I paid for my own dinner," she said breathlessly.

Matt gave a low laugh. "So you did," he conceded and, lowering his head toward her, brushed her lips in a gentle kiss. "Good night."

Wordlessly, Alison watched him stride down the hallway, his hair picking up the overhead lights so that it shone with deep brown-black glints. When he had turned the corner and was out of sight Alison unlocked her door and stepped into her room. She stood in the darkness but made no move to turn on the lights. She had suddenly realized something so extraordinary and devastating that it had literally taken her breath away.

No! She shook her head as if to banish the thought back to her subconscious from which it had come. No! It was impossible . . . ridiculous . . . unbelievable. She couldn't possibly—*she just couldn't!*

Alison's shoulders slumped and she stared into the darkness. As she had watched Matt's lithe, broad-shouldered form walk away down the hall it had come to her very simply. She loved Matt Drake. Loved him with all the force and desire of a woman who has kept her heart under lock and key and who has all but denied to herself the very existence of love. She couldn't laugh and shrug off the emotion with the composure that had belonged to an earlier Alison, or resist it as she would an infatuation. It was love with all the trimmings—adoration, jealousy, despair, sensuality, and desire.

Alison buried her head in her hands and conceded that she was beaten. Matt had won the war, all right. He had ambushed her supposedly impregnable heart so secretly that she had never even sensed the enemy approaching. And now she was helpless, vulnerable, and exposed to every hurt that Matt Drake could administer. How Karen would laugh if she could see her friend now, the cool and haughty Alison Ramsey—conquered by love!

Chapter Eight

Alison chewed on her pencil, drummed her nails on the desktop, and looked hopelessly at the blank wall in front of her. She had telephoned the promised report to George earlier in the morning, and when she had finished he had told her that the *Fairfax Courier* was interested in an article for the weekend's paper—deadline tomorrow. Alison had reorganized her notes and started to write, but to no avail. The revelation of the previous night kept coming back and back, like a bad penny.

The knowledge that she loved Matt had sent her into the depths of despair and she had spent several hours pacing in her hotel room, assuring herself that it could not be so. Finally, in utter exhaustion, she had fallen asleep and, to her surprise, had woken in relatively good spirits. She decided to take the late-afternoon plane out of Key West on the assumption that the more distance she put between Matt Drake and herself the better. Absence does not necessarily make the heart grow fonder, she argued to herself, and the sooner she could get over a man who had more women than he needed the happier she would feel.

Alison tossed her pencil onto the desk and ran her fingers through her hair. She felt hot and sweaty despite the efficient air conditioning and yearned for a cool shower. She'd write the article on the plane or when she got home to Fairfax. Now she would wash her hair, pack, and then spend a few hours enjoying the last bit of summer sunshine she was going to see for several months. Alison stripped off her sundress, threw it over a chair, and walked into the bathroom. She was just about to turn on the shower when there was a knock at the door.

"Yes?" She stuck her head around the bathroom door.

A soft female voice spoke. "It's the maid, ma'am—to change the bed."

Alison thought for a second and then shrugged. The maid could change her bed while she took a shower. "Come on in," she said.

The cool spray of the shower was a definite relief and Alison spent a long time shampooing and rinsing her hair. When she finally emerged into the steamy bathroom she could hear no sound in her room and concluded that the maid had come and gone. She dried herself, blew her hair dry, and then, wrapping a large dry towel around her, stepped into the bedroom.

"It's about time" came a voice from the main room.

A startled Alison discovered Matt, in jeans and a sports shirt, leisurely reclining on her couch, a magazine in his hand and his sneakered feet up on the coffee table. "What are you doing here?" she asked with a show of outrage. Underneath, she was trembling, and her heart was beating so loudly that she could hear it in her eardrums.

"Just making sure that the facilities are working okay." He had a wicked grin that gleamed white in his bronzed face and he did nothing to conceal the more than adequate appraisal he was making of her semi-naked body.

Alison clutched the towel tighter. "I hope you're satisfied," she said sarcastically.

"Oh, more than satisfied." His glance rested on the upper portion of her body, where her breasts curved above the line of her towel. Alison would have liked to pull the towel higher, but that would have meant risking a more extreme nudity.

With all the nonchalance she was capable of, Alison sauntered back into the bedroom and closed the door. "How did you get in here anyway?" she called through the wooden partition.

"The maid let me in."

"Isn't that against hotel regulations?" Alison inquired as she threw the towel onto the bed and began to dress.

"Bribery is so effective."

"What did you do—threaten her with losing her job?"

"Nothing so dramatic; I merely gave her the morning off and promised to make the bed myself."

Alison glanced wildly over to the double bed with its neat counterpane and blushed. "What a clever way to gain experience," she snapped. "If your firm ever goes under, you can always get a job as a maid."

Matt was not deterred by her sarcasm. "My thoughts exactly," he threw back smoothly.

Alison hastily finished dressing, pulling on a pair of beige slacks and a short-sleeved white blouse with a flowered pattern the color of cinnamon. When she finally emerged from the bedroom she found Matt standing by her desk and reading the sheet she had left in the typewriter.

"I'm glad you liked the hotel," he said, turning to face her.

"The article isn't finished," she said pointedly. "I always leave the worst until last."

Matt raised an eyebrow. "But you won't take me off your mailing list and leave me in a state of suspense?"

"You'll be the first to know," she replied sweetly.

Matt surveyed her. "You don't look ready to go snorkeling."

"Snorkeling? What are you talking about?"

"The plans we discussed last night to go snorkeling today," he said blandly.

For a moment Alison was speechless as she ran through the evening of the night before. "Matt Drake," she finally said, in an angry tone, "we never discussed snorkeling at all."

Matt made a pretense of studying the ceiling. "Perhaps you're right . . . it must have been yesterday afternoon."

"Matt!" Alison's voice was threatening.

The smile he gave her was devastatingly full of charm. "But of course you'll go anyway."

"No I won't. I'm flying out on the afternoon plane."

"And missing tonight's party?"

Alison was disconcerted. "What party?"

"Where you get to meet the person who has the final say on all my development plans."

Alison looked at Matt's innocent expression with suspicion. "And who would that be?" she asked, placing her hands on her hips.

"You have to come to the party to find out."

"I don't believe you," she retorted. "I'm sure you're the one who makes the final decisions."

"Officially, perhaps, but there *is* someone who can change my plans like that." And he snapped his fingers to demonstrate.

Alison stared at him for a second and weighed her options. He could be lying, but then he also could be telling the truth. And if he were, then as an investigative reporter she had no choice but to go along with him. "All right," she sighed. "You win—I'll stay for an extra day." She reached for the phone.

"Who are you calling?"

"The airline—to cancel my flight."

"There's no need," Matt countered as he walked toward the door. "I've already canceled it."

Alison's hand stopped in midair. "You did what?"

Matt's expression was unrepentant. "I canceled your reservation."

"But how did you know . . . ?"

"Key West has only one airline," he said smoothly, "and its reservation list is hardly a state secret. I've had Terry phoning every day. I figured that you might want to leave sooner than you should."

Alison could do no more than gape at his audacity.

"So, I'll meet you in front of the hotel in ten minutes. You'd better pack a bathing suit and towel." And with that he turned to go.

The door had already closed behind him by the time Alison's sandal had smacked against it. "Blast!" she exploded, and then heaved a sigh of resignation. All she had to endure was one more day of Matt Drake. Surely she could survive that with her sanity intact. And your virtue? the little voice inside returned. Alison retrieved her ineffectual sandal, and her shoulders drooped. Fending off the advances of Matt was not one of her favorite sports. For one thing, she always ended up competing in spite of herself; and secondly, he always won.

Matt's cabin cruiser far surpassed any boat that Alison's imagination could conceive of. It had below-deck living quarters, an above-the-deck lounge area that was roofed in the front and open in the back, and, above that, a small glassed enclosure which held the steering equipment and chairs for the boat's captain and mate.

Alison was particularly enchanted with the small, compact apartment below the deck. It had a narrow galley, complete with stove, refrigerator, sink, and cabinets. The living room had a couch and chairs, with cushions gaily decorated in orange and blue stripes, and matching curtains hung over the portholes. There was also a bedroom with a double bed and a fully equipped bathroom. Matt's boat, Alison surmised, raised sea-manship from a rugged sport into a pleasure jaunt.

As Matt had directed, Alison stowed her clothes in one of the dressers in the bedroom and then changed into her bathing suit. Then she wandered up to the level where Matt stood before the boat's wheel. They had left the pier fifteen minutes earlier and Alison could feel the steady pulsing of the ship's engines in the floor below her bare feet.

Matt had changed from his jeans into a pair of white bathing trunks and he looked like some ocean god with his bare bronzed chest, his legs planted wide apart, and his dark hair whipped by the wind. The white trunks emphasized not only his dark skin but also his narrow waist and lean hips. Alison firmly looked away and down toward the water that was rushing behind them. Key West was receding into the distance and the ocean spread around them on all sides, right up to the cloudless horizon. It was a vast expanse of bluish-green water, choppy with small waves and dotted with other pleasure craft. Above their heads sea gulls wheeled and then dove into the ocean in search of food. Some of the birds, their hunger appeased, rested on the water, bobbing in the boat's frothy wake.

"Want to try your hand at the wheel?" Matt broke into her thoughts.

Alison had barely been on a boat before, much less driven one. Motivated by curiosity, she walked over to Matt and took hold of the wheel that he had relinquished. She anticipated that driving the boat would feel like driving a car, but to her surprise the wheel pulled sharply to one side as the boat rose on a wave, and she had to struggle to straighten it and keep the boat on course.

"Having problems?" Matt, who had been standing to her side, now slipped behind her, wrapped his arms around her, and placed his hands over hers on the wheel.

Alison felt her heart lurch as his lips touched her ear and his warm cheek pressed against her hair. "Not enough to need help," she retorted, trying to step out of his grasp and ending up right against the wheel. "I thought you said that you didn't make passes in broad daylight," she said desperately.

"That was on dry land," he murmured into her hair, and his arms tightened around her like iron bands.

"Well, you're going to end up on dry land if you don't watch it," she replied tartly, and with relief she felt Matt's arms drop as he pushed her slightly to one side and grabbed the wheel. The boat, without guidance, had swerved sharply to one side and seemed intent on returning to shore. Matt's muscular arms tensed as he fought to turn the boat against the force of the waves.

Alison walked down to the open deck and sat in one of the lounge chairs. She closed her eyes, allowing the sun's rays to fall on her face. She could hear the wind, the raucous cries of the sea gulls, and the slapping sound of the water hitting the hull of the boat. The scent of seawater filled her nostrils and she could occasionally feel the ocean spray strike her skin. It was a new experience for her; she had lived all her life in a small town, landlocked by rolling hills and miles away from any body of water except a pond or a small lake. It was, she decided, something akin to heaven.

Then she felt the boat's engines slow and the wind that had been rushing through her hair melted to a breeze. "Where are we?" she called out to Matt, who was killing the engine, and pressing the button that dropped the anchor.

"At the edge of the coral reef." He went below while Alison looked over the side of the boat. A dark, hazy mass lay under the blue-green water. It seemed to stretch for miles in all directions.

Matt returned with snorkeling equipment, and Alison, taking one glance at the tangle of weighted belts, tubes, masks, and flippers, decided to throw herself on his mercy. "I can swim," she said, "but I've never snorkeled before, so if you want to go on I'll wait in—"

"Don't be ridiculous," he growled and dug through the box of equipment. "I'm going to teach you."

Matt was very thorough. Within the next half hour Alison had not only learned how to use the mask with its attached snorkel but had also been given a brief lecture on the coral reef. She was, he told her firmly, not to touch anything, no matter how interesting or enticing. Although the coral reef looked like an undersea garden, it was composed of animals, not plants, and some of them were poisonous. In addition, the reef was so fragile that if she stood on it or broke off a piece she would destroy a living organism. Florida's coral reef, Matt went on to explain, was protected by law, and all visitors were warned to treat it for what it was—a vast community of living and breathing animals that was fighting daily for survival.

"But I thought coral was a stone," Alison said in some confusion.

"The hard part of the coral is made of skeletons, but the surface is made up of thousands of living things."

Alison, outfitted and prepared, lowered herself into the water, gingerly put her mask-covered face down, and swam slowly away from the boat. For a second she could clearly see the multicolored reef below her and then her mask filled with water. She came upright, treading water madly and sputtering for all she was worth. When she pulled the mask off she found Matt beside her, laughing.

"It's not funny," she said with indignation. "My gills aren't developed enough for this."

Matt pulled her back to the boat's ladder. "A redemonstration of lesson number two: how to empty a water-filled mask."

Alison watched closely as he put his mask back on, submerged, and then came up, his mask full of water.

He squeezed the rubber indentations around his nose and, breathing outward, expelled the water from under the mask's bottom rim. The mask automatically went back to its earlier configuration when he released the pressure.

"It's simple," he said. "You can do it underwater."

"I guess I missed that lesson," Alison said ruefully and, duplicating Matt's action, submerged, came up, and emptied her mask. "Okay, here I go."

This time she managed quite well, and when she felt that she had mastered the snorkel as well, Alison concentrated on the reef below her. It was another world, so strange and enchanting that, for minutes at a time, she just floated on the surface, watching the action below.

The coral reef was more beautiful than any garden. The colors of the reef were as intense and variegated as a rainbow. Schools of fish swam in and around the waving ferns and rocks. One variety was a flashy orange and navy blue, another had stripes of indigo and gold, and still others were a deep scarlet with black spots. The reef itself was breathtaking. Ferns that Alison now knew to be animals waved to and fro with the momentum of the underwater swell. They were a bright orange or crimson and as delicate and frothy as lace.

Matt, swimming before her, pointed toward something and beckoned to her to come down. Alison took a deep breath and submerged lower. He was pointing to a coral and then to his head. Alison saw what he meant; the grayish-white curving mass looked like a human brain. A bright yellow anemone caught her eye and she decided to swim closer. Rotating with the slow-motion speed of underwater swimming, Alison came face to face with a large, white, thick-featured, and very curious fish. Startled, she just floated as he made a leisurely tour from her head to her knees before wandering off to investigate what she hoped would be more interesting phenomena.

Alison surfaced alongside Matt and they grinned at each other.

"Who was that?" she asked. "A friend of yours?"

"A grouper," Matt answered, running his hand over his wet, glistening hair. "But it seems that we have similar taste in women."

Alison submerged quickly, grateful that the ocean could camouflage her reddened cheeks. When Matt was like this—charming, teasing, and delightful—she could feel the resistant part of herself melting like ice in the hot sun. Matt had an uncanny ability to make the woman he was with feel like the only woman in the world. Alison had to constantly remind herself that he had only to crook his little finger and there were at least three women whom she could name who would come running.

Alison looked down at the waving green-gold frond of a lettuce-shaped coral. She shrugged away the disquieting thoughts and concentrated on exploring the reef. She would probably never have another chance to swim so close to a tropical reef again and she had better make the most of the opportunity. The only coral that existed in Fairfax was the pink coral necklace that belonged to George's mother's niece, Stella. Even if she asked to see it a few times, it wasn't going to equal a day swimming in the Keys.

By the end of an hour, Alison was ready to call it quits.

"Giving up so soon?" Matt surfaced alongside the boat as Alison wearily pulled herself up the ladder.

"I'm wrinkling before my time." She countered his grin with one of her own and, heaving herself over the edge of the boat, collapsed into the closest deck chair.

Matt's head, the mask pushed up into his hair, rose above the deck's edge. He eyed Alison, leaning back in the chair, flippers still on her feet and her mask dangling from one finger as her arm hung over the chair's side. "I'll make a bargain with you."

"What kind of a bargain?" Alison yawned.

"You make lunch, and I put the diving gear away."

Alison suddenly realized that she was starving. "It sounds like a fair division of labor," she conceded and then kicked off her flippers, unhooked the belt of weights from her waist, and wrapped a towel over her hair, making a turban. "Don't expect anything too glamorous."

Alison, on her first tour of the boat, had already delved into the kitchen cabinets, and now she pulled out a can of salmon and, mixing it with mayonnaise from the refrigerator, made several sandwiches. She put them on a tray with several cans of cold beer and brought them topside.

"Ta-da-de-de-um," she announced in a wicked imitation of Matt's offering of eggs Benedict the morning of his stay in Fairfax. "A mouth-watering combination of salmon, spiced with creamy mayonnaise, served on fresh slices of rye bread, to be watered down by a refreshing glass of sparkling beer."

Matt, getting the reference, smiled. "And I suppose this concoction has a title?"

"Sure," she said blithely. "Canned Salmon Sandwiches à la Alison Ramsey."

Matt winced. "You could give gourmet cooking a bad name."

After lunch, Alison and Matt companionably cleaned up the dishes in the galley kitchen. She mentioned how impressed she was with the compact layout of the boat, and Matt told her that he had designed it himself. "But I haven't named it yet," he added. "A boat, you know, should be named after a woman."

He glanced at her with a rakish look and Alison's heart seemed to falter. He was so . . . sexy standing there before her, despite the dish towel in his hand. They were side by side in the tiny kitchen and Alison could smell his clean, masculine scent and it made her feel more than a little bit dizzy.

"You shouldn't have any trouble," she finally said with asperity.

"You don't think so?" He took a step closer to her and Alison backed out of the galley and into the living room. Another menacing step on Matt's part and Alison discovered that she had been maneuvered into the bedroom.

"No, Matt—don't," she said helplessly as he pulled her into his arms and with one hand unwrapped the towel she had wound around her head. Her blond hair tumbled to her cheeks. "Why not?" he asked gently as he ran his fingers through the tangle. "I want you, Alison, and you want me."

"No, I . . ."

"I can see it in your eyes. As I said before, you have very expressive eyes." Her lids fluttered down as he kissed the corners of her eyes.

Then he took her mouth and Alison yielded, again overcome by the force of her own desires. His lips tasted slightly salty and his skin felt warm against hers. She could feel the rough grazing as the hair on his chest and legs rubbed against her bare skin and the intimate contact made her quiver.

"You see?" he murmured, lifting his head, his dark eyes gazing into her soft blue ones. Alison shook her head, unable to speak, but Matt caught her chin with his hand. "Why fight so hard against something we both want so much?" he asked with a smile and then kissed her again.

This time he ran a large, strong hand over the creamy skin of her shoulder and down the curve of her spine to the clasp of her bikini top. Although her mouth was still held firmly to his Alison tried to protest. It was too late. He had unclasped the hook that held the back closed and the top of her bathing suit fell to make a small heap on the floor at their feet.

Alison made an instinctive gesture of modesty but

Matt gently brushed her hand aside. "No," she whispered, as his head began its slow descent.

His lips brushed across her shoulder to the hollow of her throat and then down to the naked swell of her breasts. Her nipples hardened in anticipation of his touch.

Alison discovered that she could not stop him, not even when he cupped one breast in his hand and brought his mouth to its pointed, sensitive tip. Her attempted denial came out as a moan, and when he pushed her gently down onto the bed she went with him willingly, her hands running over his broad back, her lips pressed against one muscular shoulder. The feel of his taut, warm skin and the muscles rippling beneath made her senses swim and she luxuriated in his closeness . . . his bigness . . . the very masculine feel of him.

Then his hand moved from her breast to her flat stomach, which trembled under his touch. When his hand moved even lower to the band of her bikini bottom Alison regained partial control of her senses. She shook her head beneath his lips and tried to grab his arm. Matt easily pinioned her wrist and then raised it to the hand he had tucked around her shoulder. Alison, with one hand pinned under his side and the other held near her head, was now completely helpless.

"I . . . no, I can't . . ." she began breathlessly, but he stopped her words with a kiss and under the demands of his lips she seemed to slip into another world where rules and standards no longer applied, where the only thing that was important was to stay in his arms, wrapped in the warmth of his naked skin and held against the hardness of his chest.

There was a sudden lurch as the boat was bumped, and Matt's head lifted abruptly.

"Ahoy there, mate!" a voice yelled. "Is anyone there?"

Matt cursed and then took a deep breath. "Sorry, darling," he murmured, running his finger over her lips in a light, quick caress. Then he got up and walked over to the open porthole at the far end of the bedroom. "What's the matter?" he called out.

"Sorry to bother you, mate," the voice called back as the two boats smacked together again, "but our engine's gone on the blink and I was wondering if you could tow us back to shore when you go."

"Just a minute." Matt pulled his head back in and glanced at Alison, who had pulled the bedspread over her in a protective gesture. He grimaced and then left the room, shutting the bedroom door behind him.

Alison lay on the bed, limp as a rag doll and not certain whether to laugh or cry at the irony of her situation. Because she loved Matt every defense that had guarded her in the past had now crumbled. She was a far cry from the proud, untouchable Alison of only a month ago. Now she was protected by only the flimsiest of shields: fate. And she knew with certainty that the next time she found herself half-naked in bed with Matt Drake fate, unreliable as always, would desert her.

The worst part of it, Alison reflected sadly, was that he didn't love her in return. What had he said? I want you and you want me. A nice, simple formula. X equals Y—so why not get into bed together? Alison bit her lip. She still didn't want sex without love, affection, marriage, and the future commitment of a family. She was hopelessly old-fashioned, no matter how modern her physical desires had become. She could sleep with Matt and satisfy one need, but all the rest would remain unfulfilled.

Alison rose and got out her clothes. All she had to do was endure one more evening in Matt's company. She would go to the party, plead a headache, retire early, and then take the morning flight out of Key West. With any luck, she could return to Fairfax and easily regain the Alison Ramsey she had always known.

Chapter Nine

When the knock sounded on her door Alison was putting the finishing touches on her makeup. "Just a minute," she called out. Her lipstick went into her purse, her gray skirt was straightened with a tug, and Alison stilled her heart to answer the door.

Matt leaned against the doorway, dressed in a dark tuxedo and a white silk shirt with ruffles down the front. He looked debonair and very, very handsome, and Alison was surprised to find that the combination of masculinity and ruffles was more attractive than she had ever expected. Then the significance of the tuxedo hit her, and she glanced down uncertainly at her modestly tailored gray suit.

"Terry said that your suitcase was so small that she was sure you hadn't packed a proper dress," Matt said as she looked up at him again.

"But I didn't know . . . I had no idea that the party would be formal."

Matt walked in, tucked his hand under Alison's elbow, and planted a gentle kiss on the center part in her silvery blond hair. "A fair damsel in distress," he joked, "and Matt Drake to the rescue."

Alison was too flustered by his kiss to pull away as he led her firmly out of the room and down the corridor to the elevator. "But if it's formal, then I can't go. Why don't you go without me?" she finally suggested. "It's no problem—I'll just stay here tonight."

"Nonsense," Matt said crisply, directing her into the open elevator. "A solution to the problem is at hand."

"What solution?" Alison tried discreetly to tug her arm out of Matt's strong grasp but to no avail.

Matt waited until the elevator had settled at the main floor. As the doors opened and then closed behind them he turned to her. "I'm taking you to La Ronde. Danielle will have the perfect dress."

"No!" This time she made no attempt to be discreet. His grip on her elbow tightened and she remained trapped.

"You don't want to have the proper dress?"

Alison denied that as they passed out of the hotel's main doors and into Matt's gleaming steel-gray Ferrari. "I do, but . . ." Her voice trailed off as Matt turned his key in the ignition. How could she explain to someone of Matt's financial caliber that one designer original from La Ronde would pay her food bill for a year?

Matt seemed to have read her mind. As the car leaped powerfully forward he said in a casual tone, "Don't worry about the cost."

"What do you mean—don't worry about the cost? I'm a working girl, remember?"

"It's my gift."

"Oh, no." Alison shook her head decisively. She knew all about Matt's gifts. They came with strings attached—amorous strings. Kisses for payment; love-making to settle a debt. She couldn't emotionally afford to be the recipient of Matt's financial largesse.

The Ferrari drew up before La Ronde's elegant brick façade. "You can't go in that suit. I know you'll feel out of place."

"Then I just won't go."

"And miss meeting . . . ?" He paused.

"Meeting who?" Alison quickly rejoined. "Who is this mysterious authority of yours?"

"Let's put it this way. If you can persuade this person that I shouldn't build the resort, then there's a chance that it won't get built." One dark eyebrow arched mockingly as Matt watched the expressions that passed over Alison's face. He knew full well that he had offered her the ultimate bribe, she reflected grimly.

Alison opened her mouth and then shut it again. She wanted to say that she didn't care, but the words wouldn't come out. She wanted to puncture his confidence and then watch his ego deflate. She wanted to . . . blast! She wanted to meet this unknown man who wielded such influence over Matt's decisions. It would be her last opportunity to stop Matt's firm from eventually turning Fairfax into a town of souvenir shops and fast-food restaurants. If she didn't go to the party strangers would be walking along Main Street next winter, their cars clogging the thoroughfares and their money altering Fairfax beyond recognition.

Alison looked down at her hands. "I'll pay you in monthly installments for the dress."

Matt eyed her downturned profile for a moment. "All right," he said easily and then moved quickly and lithely from the car.

Alison was surprised at his quick acceptance. She knew Matt too well to have anticipated that he would capitulate so easily. As he opened her door and helped her out she eyed him suspiciously. She had a feeling that Matt had something up his sleeve, but his chiseled features were set in a bland, enigmatic expression and she knew that she would have to wait to discover what motives underlay his strange behavior.

Danielle's shop was every bit as luxurious as Alison remembered, and when the older woman came out of a back room, her arms extended in welcome, she was just as beautiful as Alison's earlier impression had led her to believe. Any wrinkles were cleverly concealed by skillfully applied makeup, and Danielle's fair complexion and wide green eyes were as fresh-looking as a young girl's.

"How delightful, Matt! You can't visit too often for me, you know."

Matt kissed her cheek. "We have to outfit Alison for the party tonight. She didn't know that she was going to be attending a formal affair."

Danielle welcomed her with more warmth than Alison would have expected from an ex-lover of Matt's and then eyed her in a shrewd, professional way. Alison was occupied with pondering Matt's statement. It was evident that Danielle would be going to the party as well. Alison wondered how many of Matt's girl friends, new and old, would be in attendance. If it weren't for the mystery man Matt had promised to introduce her to, Alison would have turned on her heel and walked out of La Ronde right then. She wanted no part of an evening where the competition for her escort's attention would be so fierce.

Matt's hand was resting on her waist, and his touch brought back a memory of the afternoon's lovemaking. Alison glanced at him through her lashes. What did he think about their interrupted amorous session? Had he just wiped it out of his mind? Was it such common practice to him that he had never given it another thought? After all, Alison reasoned, with his many girl friends, bed partners were a dime a dozen. Whatever frustrations he had developed during the afternoon would, no doubt, be satisfied elsewhere.

Certainly he had hardly spoken to her for the rest of the day, although Alison had to concede that he had been busy. The other boat, with its failed engine, was a large, heavy yacht, far bigger than Matt's cabin cruiser. Knowing that it was going to be an effort to tow the other boat several miles back to shore, Matt had suggested that he take a look at the engine. He had struggled for two hot, steamy hours while Alison kept him supplied with cold beer. The yacht's owner had been useless, claiming that machinery was a mystery to him. When the engine had finally roared back to life his thanks to Matt had been profuse, but in spite of Matt's explanations he never seemed to realize what the problem had been or how Matt had solved it.

Matt had been polite to his face, but after the yacht had steamed off he had spoken a few choice words under his breath. Then he had wiped his greasy, blackened hands on the towel Alison had offered and wearily suggested that they return to Key West. He made no mention of what had taken place in the bedroom below, and she had been thankful for what she presumed was his tactfulness. But when he had left her in the hotel lobby, saying that she should be ready at seven for the party that night, Alison had gone to her room with that now familiar feeling of despondency. Wasn't she glad Matt hadn't tried to resume their lovemaking? She didn't want to have to fight off his advances again, did she?

"I think something flowing, yet quietly elegant," Danielle was saying to Matt. "Something that would set off her blondness."

Matt was nodding his head in agreement and Alison found herself ushered into a large, luxurious changing room with a gold carpet, mirrored walls, and an opaque screen in one corner. As she slipped out of her suit and hung it neatly on a hanger Danielle bustled in with several dresses. She eyed Alison's slim half-dressed figure and shook her head. "Too big," she muttered and went out again. Alison felt distinctly odd. She was used to shopping in the kind of store where she made the selection, brought the dresses into a dressing room, and tried them on all by herself. She wasn't used to the personal approach or the glamorous ambiance of a haute couture shop.

Danielle returned with another set of dresses and

hung them on a hook. "Try this one first," she said, indicating a pale blue chiffon with spaghetti straps and an Empire waistline.

The dress was long, well cut, and flowing, and Alison, swiveling in the mirror, thought that she looked very nice. The door to the changing room opened and she turned to see Matt coming in. To her surprise, he sat down on one of the gold velvet chairs and looked her over.

"What do you think?" Danielle asked.

Alison was about to say that the dress was fine when she realized that the older woman was not speaking to her. Matt shook his dark head. "Too much the ingenue," he said decisively and Danielle nodded in agreement.

Alison was ordered to go behind the screen and try on another dress. She went through several, each more glamorous than the last. She avoided asking about the prices, which were nowhere in evidence. Presumably Danielle's usual clientele had no need to worry about cost. Alison did, but she was already quite nervous enough at having a man choose her clothes, and having her assets and flaws discussed as if she weren't present, without looking for one more thing to worry about.

The last gown in the pile was a deep burgundy confection that Alison was sure wouldn't suit her. She was accustomed to wearing pastels and light colors; this was too deep, too dark, and too dramatic. But she knew better than to say so; Danielle and Matt had already insisted that she try each dress on, no matter what she thought. With a sigh, she put the dress over her head and then pulled up the tiny zipper in the back. With a final adjustment of the skirt she emerged into the changing room and Matt whistled, not a catcall but a low, admiring sound.

Alison flushed, turned, and then gasped. Surely the woman in the mirror couldn't be her? She had the same blond hair, the same dark-lashed aquamarine eyes and fair complexion, but there the resemblance stopped. The rest of the woman was sexy and provocative in a way that Alison Ramsey from Fairfax could never be. Her breasts, creamy against the burgundy silk, swelled out above the plunging neckline. The bodice was made of panels, each one cut in a triangle pointing to her waist. The result was a deceptively small waistline—no bigger than a girl's. From there the wine-red silk seductively swathed her slim hips and then flared out just above her knees to the floor. When she walked the skirt swirled around her ankles with the rich sound that only silk can make.

"Well?" Danielle asked, her hands on her hips, her eyes gauging the dress's every line.

"Turn around," Matt ordered, and Alison obediently swiveled, showing him first the V-cut décolletage and then the deep-cut back, which left her spine bare all the way to her waist. "Perfect," he murmured, and his voice was a warm caress that made Alison shiver.

Alison tried to protest but neither Danielle nor Matt would listen. She was assured that the dress fit her perfectly and that the color was just right for her. Alison wanted to say that it was the style that was unsuitable—the wine-red silk exposed her charms almost to the point of no return. She wasn't used to wearing such a provocative dress; even the blue dress she had purchsed on her last visit to Key West had a high neckline.

"What is the cost of this dress?" she said hesitantly as Danielle gathered up the other clothes.

"That's a custom-made dress, dear, and—"

Matt interrupted smoothly. "Danielle will send me a bill, Alison. Don't worry about it."

Alison was silent. A look had passed between Matt and the older woman, and she guessed that they had made some kind of agreement. She suspected that she wouldn't find out the price, no matter how hard she tried. The fact that Matt and Danielle Chenier were in cahoots made her more certain than ever that Matt had something up his sleeve. She made a gesture of resignation and Matt laughed softly. "You look beautiful," he said and led her out of the changing room.

Her suit was packed in a box and deposited in the trunk of the Ferrari. Danielle kissed them both goodbye and said that she would see them later. She had kept the shop open late for their benefit, and now she would get changed herself. As Matt drove the Ferrari through the twisting streets that characterized the island's wealthy suburban tracts Alison stared out her window into the gathering dusk. She had the uneasy feeling that things were happening behind her back. She remembered the way Terry had noticed her tiny suitcase but made no mention that she would be going to a formal party. Why hadn't Matt told her when he was in Fairfax? Was it because he had thought that she would refuse to go? Alison frowned. What was Matt up to? She couldn't make heads or tails out of any of it.

The Ferrari pulled into a long gravel driveway that curved up to the doors of the Key West Club, a long, rambling stone building with an impressively carved stone entrance. Matt helped Alison out of the car and handed the keys to an attendant. They were ushered into a large foyer, lit with chandeliers and filled with elegantly dressed men and women in tuxedos and formal gowns. Matt had been right about one thing, Alison conceded. If she had insisted on wearing her suit she would have stuck out like a sore thumb.

"Matt, my dear." The voice that spoke was imperious and Alison turned to find Matt leaning down to kiss the hand of a woman in a wheelchair. "And this, of course, must be Alison."

Alison looked at her in surprise and then recognized the face with its crown of gray braids. "You must be Matt's aunt," she said with a smile.

"Yes, my child."

For a moment the two women took stock of each

other. Despite the wheelchair and her fragility, Elizabeth Schwarzenville was regal and dignified, wearing a long white mantilla that fell over the shoulders of her gray silk dress. The braids framed a face that was wrinkled but filled with serenity, and her deep blue eyes were clear and keen. She took hold of Alison's hand with her small beringed fingers and perused her face. The older woman's eyes seemed to notice everything and Alison had the sensation that Elizabeth could see below her sophisticated, glamorous façade to the Alison below, an Alison who was confused, frightened, and out of her depth. Perhaps—and Alison drew back slightly—she could even see into that inner place in Alison's heart where her love for Matt lay like a tiny, closed seed.

"Matt has told me all about you."

"He . . . he has?" Alison glanced up to look at Matt only to discover that he had slipped away into the crowd, leaving Alison alone with this tiny but formidable woman.

"Of course—and I intend to find out more myself."

"But Matt . . ."

"Matt knows that I wish to talk to you, child. If you'll wheel me down the hall, then we might find a private corner where we can converse."

Alison could do nothing but obey. She wheeled the older woman out of the crowded foyer and down a long carpeted corridor. As the noise behind them receded the older woman gave a sigh. "I love parties," she said, "but I love peace more." She indicated a door with one hand and Alison pushed it open, pulling the wheelchair in after her. They had entered the library, an empty and impressive room with many bookshelves, high carved wooden ceilings, and deep leather wing chairs.

"Now, sit down, Alison, so we can really talk."

Alison obediently sank into one of the leather chairs, nervously smoothing the deep red silk of her dress over her knees. "Mrs. Schwarzenville . . ."

"Please call me Elizabeth." The old woman paused

for a moment and surveyed Alison's confused expression. "I think you have something to ask me."

Alison stared at Elizabeth blankly and then a sudden realization dawned on her. "Am I supposed to ask *you* about the hotel?"

Elizabeth nodded, her hands quiet in her lap.

"But . . . but why?" When Matt had mentioned a higher authority Alison had expected to meet a banker or some other business executive whose choice would be based on financial concerns. She had never anticipated that his decision to invest millions might depend upon the opinion of an old woman, no matter with what esteem he regarded her.

Elizabeth's deep blue eyes gazed serenely at her. "You didn't expect it would be me, did you?" Alison nodded slowly. "Matt does not rely on me for monetary judgments, my child, but for moral ones. Your concerns about Fairfax have worried him, and he has asked me to consider if your objections are valid."

"But"—Alison swallowed—"could you be fair? After all, Matt is your nephew."

"That is true." The head with its crown of braids dipped regally. "But I am much too old and crochety to worry that any decision that I make will cause Matt to turn against me. I have no need of his money, and he knows that my perception of his success comes not from his financial standing but from the rightness of his choices."

Alison sat in her chair for a long and silent moment. With a word, this tiny woman could influence a decision that would change her life, the lives of her friends, and the character of Fairfax. She looked up to find Elizabeth's eyes resting on her. They were filled with intelligence, honesty, and inner peace, and Alison suddenly felt a weight lift from her shoulders. It was the weight of Fairfax and of unknown possibilities. It was the weight of fights and conflicts, both with Matt and with the town council. Alison sensed the other woman's integrity and realized that she would be fair and unbiased. Yes, she suddenly decided, she would like to tell Matt's aunt about Fairfax.

Alison launched into her story. She told the older woman all about the town—its history, the people she had grown up with, and the manner of small-town life. She concealed nothing. Fairfax had economic difficulties, but they could be solved with alternative solutions, Alison argued, that would not bring strangers into their town. Perhaps a computer industry could be enticed to establish a base in Fairfax; its employees would become town members, not transients who would care nothing for the value of property or the town's population.

Alison even delved into the personal. She told about the party the town housing committee had thrown for her father on his retirement. She told how she had started working at the station for George Birch's father, and that now she was working for George. She told Elizabeth about Karen, Jeremy, and baby Carrie. She even mentioned Samson, who had been found wandering down Main Street, a tiny kitten without its mother. The town druggist had picked him up and called Alison, who had a well-known soft spot for animals.

"You see, we all know each other. It's like being a part of a large, warm family. Oh, I know that sometimes it gets a bit claustrophobic, and every town has its personality problems, but Fairfax is special to me . . ." Alison's voice trailed off and she stared at her hands.

"You would make a good lawyer, child." Elizabeth finally spoke. "You've made a good case for your town, and your love for it tells me that your own heart is very big. I will think about what you have said, about what Matt has told me, and look at my photographs."

Alison's head came up. "Photographs?"

"Matt took photographs of Fairfax for me. Since I cannot travel, he functions as my eyes. I have over a hundred pictures of your town—even of your house. I am beginning to feel as if I know Fairfax very well." She stopped and then looked shrewdly at Alison. "And now, my child, what about you and Matt?"

Alison stiffened. "I don't know what you mean."

The deep blue eyes were very perceptive. "I have no desire to pry into the affairs of your heart, Alison, but Matt means a great deal to me."

"He's . . . he's just a friend." Alison stared at the toe of her sandaled foot as it peeked out from under the hem of her dress.

"I see." There was a moment of silence as Elizabeth looked at Alison's profile. "Then perhaps as a friend you might be interested in hearing about Matt's childhood?"

The question hung in the air between them until Alison finally looked back at her.

"Yes," she said softly.

Elizabeth Schwarzenville looked away from Alison and out a nearby window. "When my sister was dying she begged me to come from Switzerland, and when I came she pleaded with me to bring up her children after her death. I had just been through a painful divorce, and I badly needed a family to give me a sense of belonging. Matt was five and Jane was two then. I had no children of my own, and in my loneliness I welcomed this ready-made motherhood." Elizabeth paused, as if to collect her resources.

"So you agreed?"

"Yes, I agreed. My sister died happier, I think, knowing that someone from her family would participate in the development of her children."

Alison nodded her head in understanding.

Elizabeth continued. "Matt was old enough to understand a great deal at the time of his mother's death. His father's lack of caring and attention hurt him, and to this day he is very resentful, although he will be the first to admit that his father has been very generous in passing his business into Matt's hands. But his parents' relationship has made him very wary of marriage, Alison, and you must be patient."

Alison was startled by the older woman's last words. "Marriage?"

Elizabeth smiled slightly. "You don't think that is possible?"

"No." Alison's voice was vehement. "Matt and I . . . we don't have that kind of relationship. As I said, we're just friends."

"Ah, yes." Elizabeth nodded her head gravely. "That is what you said." Her dark blue eyes regarded Alison's pink-cheeked face. "If you don't mind, then, we shall go back to the party. I think I have monopolized your company enough for one evening."

Alison wheeled Elizabeth out of the library and back down the long corridor to a large reception room where the guests had gathered for a buffet dinner. Elizabeth ordered Alison to wheel her over to one of the tables that had been set with white tablecloths and floral arrangements. When Alison objected because no one else was seated there, Elizabeth laughed. "This is where I hold court, child. As soon as you go the guests will all come to me, one by one. I'm afraid that I'm not just an old lady who can enjoy her leisure. For some reason, I've developed into an institution—like the newspaper's advice column."

Alison left Elizabeth reluctantly, but when she looked back she saw an older couple approaching the table. The older woman had, Alison realized, a magnetism that came from serenity and wisdom. Certainly she had seen into Alison's inner heart and the desire that lay hidden there. Of course she wanted to marry Matt—she loved him. But she was a realist, too. They were incompatible. She could never live with a man who used women as if they were toys, mere items to be purchased.

Alison spotted Matt sitting at one of the tables with a crowd of people and slipped into the empty chair beside him. "Did you have a good talk with Elizabeth?" he murmured in her ear, his words covered by the animated conversation that occupied the table.

"Very," she said tartly.

"Did you convince her to decide against the hotel?"

"I hope so." Alison smiled sweetly at him and he grinned back at her, one dark eyebrow arched mockingly. They were still antagonists, fighting over the future of Fairfax with any weapons they could muster. Alison felt triumphant. If Matt thought that his lovemaking had made her retreat from her stance he was sadly mistaken. She hadn't yielded one single inch.

Matt introduced her to everyone sitting at the table. The names slipped past her so quickly that Alison doubted if she would remember any of them. ". . . and you know John Brennan—and this is his wife, Martha . . ." The dark-haired woman gave her a pleasant smile. Matt pointed to another couple. "This is an old school friend of mine, Bob Jamison, and his wife, Sandy. And of course you know Deanna."

Alison did indeed. Deanna, elegant in an ivory gown that enhanced her dark beauty, was sitting on the other side of Matt. She gave Alison a scathing, angry glance and her eyes rested on Alison's exposed cleavage with a derisive look that made Alison feel decidedly uncomfortable. What's a country bumpkin like you, Deanna's look seemed to ask, doing in a dress designed for a fashion model? Alison flushed slightly and sat back in her chair so that Matt's comforting bulk stood between her and Deanna's acid glance.

"Hey, Matt," John Brennan called out. "Bob tells me that he played the practical joke of the century on you."

Matt looked up. "He tried," he said lightly.

At the group's insistence Bob agreed to tell the story, his round face splitting into a wide grin. "Well, about a month ago, this gorgeous blonde showed up at my travel agency, asking where the night life was in Key West."

Someone hooted. "So you decided to give her a personal tour."

"No way! I've got a jealous wife."

"That's right," Sandy said, a smile lighting up her pixie face. "I always tell him—one false step and"—she drew one hand across her throat as if it were a knife—"it's curtains."

When the laughter subsided, Bob went on. "I couldn't see letting this . . . er, lovely opportunity go to waste, and immediately an inspiration came to my mind. What about my old buddy and bachelor friend, Matt—the lady-killer? So I told this very attractive blonde"—and Bob's hands drew some suggestive curves in the air to the accompaniment of several catcalls—"to be at the Pavillon at seven that night."

Alison's eyes widened as realization began to dawn on her. Quickly she looked up at Matt, who was leaning back in his chair, his arms crossed, an expression of indifference on his face.

"I made arrangements with Henri for a table for two and told him that Matt was expecting to dine with a young lady that night—a blonde in a blue dress. In the meantime, I told Matt that Sandy and I wanted to meet him at the Pavillon at seven."

Alison glanced down at her hands, her back rigid as she waited to hear the rest of Bob's story. She swallowed painfully, her throat as dry as sand. That night in Key West she'd inadvertently walked into the machinations of a practical joker. If only she hadn't been so impetuous! If only she had stayed in the condominium and played rummy with her neighbor!

Bob continued. "When Matt arrived in the lobby that night, I made my apologies to him, saying that I had substituted a very lovely lady to take our places. He was, I must say, not amused." There was laughter as the group looked at a nonchalant Matt. "Not even when I mentioned all of her . . . er, enchanting attributes. Still, I counted on Matt not to let the lady down, and under my eloquent persuasion"—more laughter; the crowd obviously knew Bob very well—"the gentleman in him prevailed. After all, it isn't nice to leave a . . . uh, lady in the lurch."

"And . . . ?" someone prompted.

"So in he went. I decided to hide behind a fern in the lobby and watch them come out after dinner. Where, I asked myself, would my bachelor friend take his lovely date after dinner?"

More catcalls and whistles. "No doubt this information is essential for the tours you organize on Key West," John Brennan teased.

"Absolutely," Bob agreed with a grin. "I'm thinking of starting a Bachelors' Special. Anyway, there I was behind the fern, when the blonde came sauntering in—half an hour late, like most women."

This comment brought a round of booing from the women present. Alison was thankful that Bob's narrative was holding his audience spellbound. She, for one, felt like sinking under the table and dying of shame. She didn't dare look at Matt. She had accused him more than once of using call girls, all based on their first meeting, and now she felt sick. She had misjudged him entirely.

"The blonde went into the restaurant and then, five minutes later, came out furious. I had to run out to the street to catch up with her. When I asked her what happened all I got were some very unladylike expressions and a dirty look. I figured that Matt must have kicked her out—she *was* a bit on the brassy side . . ."

"I bet . . ." Sandy muttered.

". . . so I went home, but I was curious to know what had happened and phoned the Pavillon. Henri assured me that Monsieur Drake was dining with a very lovely blonde lady. For a moment you could have knocked me over with a feather, but then I had the call switched to Matt and told him that he had a case of mistaken identity. It didn't seem to phase him in the least. The next day Henri told me that Monsieur Drake and the beautiful blonde had left together, but my bachelor friend here won't admit a thing."

The table's attention switched to Matt and there were a lot of knowing smiles.

"Come on, Matt, tell us what happened."

"Was she good?"

"Give us a break—how about a few hints?"

Although Alison could see Matt's jaw muscles tensing, his voice was casual. "My lips are sealed."

There were several groans. "No need to act the gentleman," someone volunteered. "Remember Bob's travel agency? He needs to know where you took the lady afterward."

"Discretion," Matt quoted lightly, "is the better part of valor."

Alison felt her face flame and she leaned forward to sip the water that stood on the table near her. She didn't know who it belonged to and she didn't care. Her throat was now so dry that she thought it might crack. When she put the glass down and looked up she discovered Deanna staring at her.

"I think," Deanna began smoothly, her voice sly, and Alison's heart plummeted to the tips of her high-heeled sandals, "that I know the identity of this elusive blonde."

"Leave it to Deanna," Bob said with a tone of delight. "It takes one woman to know another."

"It was you, Alison, wasn't it?" Deanna leaned forward, her cold glance meeting Alison's horrified one.

"Alison has never been in Key West before. You'll have to guess again," Matt interjected smoothly.

175

"But—" John Brennan looked confused and gave Alison a strange look. "I thought you said that you had been here . . ."

"Let me tell you about the joke I pulled on Bob about a week ago." Matt's voice cut across John Brennan's, and Bob groaned theatrically.

The group's attention shifted to Matt, their interest in Alison gone. She slumped in her chair, her heart still pounding, her mind whirling. Although Matt had successfully switched the conversation to a less embarrassing topic, Alison knew that the group at the table, John Brennan and Deanna in particular, had not been deceived. And although Matt had gallantly tried to conceal what had happened, Alison felt that he had implicated her further, his air of mystery giving credibility to the belief that they had made love afterward.

Alison felt Deanna's eyes on her and a brief glance at the other woman confirmed her worst suspicions. Deanna's glacial smile said it all. She thought that Alison was Matt's mistress. She thought that Alison had come all the way from Fairfax not to gain information about the hotel but to . . . to . . . Alison suddenly knew that she had to get out.

"Excuse me," she said to no one in particular and slipped away from the table. Matt was too busy with his anecdote to notice.

Alison didn't breathe freely until she was out of the foyer and standing beside the driveway. The attendant was kind enough to retrieve her suit from the Ferrari and to hail her a taxi. As she was driven back to the hotel Alison made some quick decisions. She would change, finish her packing, and take the midnight bus to Miami. From there she could get a quick plane to upstate New York. Matt, trying to track her down, would never guess that she would leave by a more time-consuming route than the direct flight from Key West.

Alison just prayed that it would take time for Matt to

discover that she had left the club. She desperately wanted to get away. She wanted no part of Matt Drake. She had done the best that she could do for Fairfax, and now all that she wanted was to get home, where life was uncomplicated by questions of love, sex, and Martin Matthew Edwards Drake.

Chapter Ten

"Miss Ramsey, will you lift me up?"

Alison looked down at the towhead of Cathie Marks and winced inwardly. It was the umpteenth time she would be lifting a child to the lower bar of the uneven parallel bars and her arms felt like dead weights. "Sure, honey," she said and, wrapping her arms around the little girl's waist, hoisted her up. She spotted her as Cathie tried to perform a hip circle and then caught her before she fell to the ground.

"Maybe I'll be able to do it next week," Cathie said wistfully.

"Of course you will," Alison replied with more confidence than she felt. She had been coaching the Fairfax gymnastics team for several years, but this season made her want to throw in the towel. The team's performance had gone from bad to worse. They had been resoundingly defeated in their last meet with the team from the neighboring town. Alison hadn't expected victory, but she had anticipated a better showing.

Alison shook her head slowly as she noticed that another one of the floor mats had a torn seam that looked beyond repair. Her team didn't lack for spirit, but they were practicing on inadequate equipment and they desperately needed another coach. Money was the problem. A recent attempt at fund raising had brought dismal results. The town's businessmen all complained of poor times and predicted worse to come.

Alison hated to admit it, but Matt's words—that Fairfax was dying—seemed to have been prophetic. In her heart, Alison knew that she had been viewing the town through rose-colored glasses, telling herself and anyone who would listen that Fairfax was prosperous, growing, and happy. She had been blind and deaf to any evidence that pointed to the contrary.

Alison sighed deeply and moved to help another little girl work on a back flip. She had managed to leave Key West without being detected and had arrived home a week before. It had been snowing, overcast, and gloomy ever since—a fitting match to her own disposition. She had thrown herself into her work and had avoided Karen and George. Alison was still confused, not to mention ashamed and embarrassed, and she didn't want to talk about Key West to anyone.

She hadn't heard from Matt since her return. Her phone had been silent and the mail had been dull, only a letter from an old school friend and several bills. As the days passed Alison grew increasingly despondent and hopeless. Matt's silence indicated what she had known all along—that his interest in her had been merely a passing fancy. An earlier Alison would have shrugged her shoulders and gone on her merry way, but this new Alison was wretched. She even spent wakeful hours at night, crying into her pillow. It was ludicrous, horrible, and humiliating that Alison Ramsey could be so miserable over a man.

"Is it time for our warm-downs, Miss Ramsey?"

Alison started and then realized that her attention had wandered far from the gym. She glanced at her watch. "Thanks, Robin." She tugged on the older girl's braids. "Why don't you start the girls on their exercises?"

"Okay." Robin beamed and started to walk away.

"Oh, and, Miss Ramsey, a man just came in. I think he wants to talk to you."

Alison whirled around to face the doorway and felt her heart leap into her throat. Matt stood there in boots, jeans, and a sheepskin jacket.

Alison walked toward him, only too aware that she couldn't have looked worse if she had tried. She wore her usual coaching outfit—a faded green leotard and a pair of scruffy green running-suit pants with white stripes down the sides. She was hot, sweaty, and exhausted, and her hair hadn't been combed for hours.

"Matt, how . . . ?" Her voice trailed off as she regarded his haggard face, with deep lines etched from his nose to his mouth.

"You're a real sight for sore eyes," he remarked jauntily, despite his obvious fatigue. "It's a good thing that green is my favorite color." And he leaned toward her in an unmistakable way.

"No! Not in front of the girls!" Alison put up a restraining hand and quickly backed away. "I . . . we have to do exercises."

When the warm-down exercises were finished Matt mobilized a cleanup crew. To Alison's amazement the girls obeyed his orders with no complaining and a great deal of giggling. His masculine charm, she noticed wryly, worked just as well on little girls as on bigger ones. And when it was time for the girls to go home he gallantly offered Jeanine, who lived two doors down from Alison, a ride. Jeanine, whose greatest moment of glory in the past had been her twice-weekly ride home with the coach, accepted his offer with alacrity, not even glancing at Alison. It was amazing, Alison decided with chagrin, how quickly children's loyalties could change.

And animals were no better. Samson was positively estatic over Matt's return and made an idiot of himself, meowing to be picked up and purring madly when Matt finally gathered him into his arms. Alison slammed and banged in the kitchen as she made coffee, muttering under her breath about disloyalty and ingratitude. By the time she went into the living room carrying a tray of cups and utensils she had worked herself up into a state of total irritation.

The scene in the living room did nothing to soothe her. Matt had built a fire that threw a warm light over the furniture. He had settled onto the couch, put his stockinged feet on the coffee table, and had Samson curled in his lap. Anyone else would have been warmed by this domestic coziness, but Alison was not. Matt had a relaxed and completely-at-home look that set her teeth on edge.

"I owe you an apology," she said curtly, slamming the tray down on the table so hard that the cups and saucers bounced.

Matt merely arched an eyebrow.

"I was wrong to accuse you of hiring . . . call girls." Alison abruptly sat down in one of the armchairs. For some reason the apology seemed to make her knees turn to water—a physical reaction that, she was sure, had nothing to do with the gleam in Matt's dark eyes. She lifted her chin defiantly. "But you were at fault, too. You knew I wasn't the girl Bob had sent."

"I know, but I just couldn't resist. And if you could have seen your face in that bedroom after you saw my sister's nightgown . . ." Matt threw back his head and laughed.

Alison picked up a cup of coffee and glared at him over its rim. He could afford to laugh. She was the one who had been made to look the fool. The double standard still prevailed. His reputation hadn't been harmed in the least. She, on the other hand, was probably considered by all his friends to be the kind of woman who made a habit of one-night stands.

"Alison, you know why I've come, don't you?"

181

She looked up at him, surprised by the odd tone in his voice. Something flickered in his eyes, but Alison attributed it to the leaping flames of the fire reflected there. She looked back at her coffee. "You've come to tell me that you're still going to build the hotel."

Matt jumped up and raked his dark hair with his fingers. "Is that the only thing you ever think about?" he growled, looking down at her.

"It's true, isn't it?" she insisted stubbornly, looking away from the hard lines of his face.

"Yes," he said harshly and then strode roughly over to the fire, where he gazed into the flames.

"I didn't convince Elizabeth at all, did I?" Alison placed her cup back on the tray and looked down at her hands.

"No. She saw too much evidence that Fairfax was in desperate need of new industry." His tone was cold and businesslike.

Alison gave an unconscious sigh. It was hard to face defeat and even harder to admit that she had been wrong in the first place. The fight against the resort had been part of her for so long that she would feel empty without it. And then there was her pride. She didn't want to tell Matt that the truth was on his side. She pondered her choices. She knew that the resort would inevitably be built, and she knew that it would bring Matt to Fairfax in the future. It didn't matter that her love for him wasn't returned, or that her desire for him was an ache that wouldn't go away. She couldn't hide from their inevitable meetings. Could they at least be friends instead of implacable enemies? If she yielded gracefully, might that not be a beginning? Alison swallowed and turned. "Matt, you were right . . ."

He turned abruptly. "I'm sorry I had to be the one to bring the bad news," he said, his jaw clenched. He was at the closet and had his jacket on before Alison grasped what he was about to do.

She stood up, almost overturning the tray with her knees. "You don't understand," she began desperately.

"I understand everything," he interrupted in a glacial voice. "I understand that you prefer to live in your own little world and remain blind to the needs and wants of others. You can't see the forest for the trees, not on the subject of Fairfax or anything else." Then he was out the door.

Alison was galvanized into action when the house shook with the slam. She ran to the door and threw it open. "Matt!" she cried.

The wind picked up the sound of her voice and carried it into the darkness. Matt never even slowed down and Alison, shivering in the cold, ran down the path toward him. "Matt!"

Did he pause for a second? Later, Alison was never able to decide whether it was his pause or her own determined run that brought her to his side before he reached the curb next to his car. "Matt?" She looked up at his harsh profile and then, hesitantly, reached out and touched his arm.

Matt turned to look down at her. On the dark street, lit only by lampposts, his face assumed a dark, brooding quality, the hollows deeper, the eyes black, his mouth set in a grim line. "What?" he asked in a forbidding tone.

"Matt, I . . . I just wanted to say . . ." She paused to catch her breath and then despaired of continuing. This wasn't the way she wanted to apologize—as if they were two strangers meeting in the night. Her courage failed her. "I have a . . . check for you."

"A check!"

"An installment for the dress."

He shrugged. "I'm not interested." And he started to turn away.

Alison shuddered as a cold gust of wind lifted her hair from her cheeks. She reached out for his arm. "I want to pay for it," she insisted desperately.

"Alison, you're an idiot," Matt said fiercely, and then suddenly he pulled her into his arms, his lips pressing remorselessly down on hers.

When his head lifted Alison gasped and then said, in a choking voice, "I owe you the money."

Matt's hands clenched her arms and he shook her. "You must be the most stubborn woman who ever walked the face of the earth. Do you have to be told that my woman doesn't have to pay for her clothes?"

"I . . . your . . . I don't understand," Alison stammered, frightened by the blaze in his eyes.

"Do I have to spell it out for you? Haven't you realized yet where our relationship is headed?"

Her lips felt stiff from the cold. "You want me to be your mistress."

"I want you to be my wife!" he roared. "For heaven's sake, do I have to go down on my knees and beg in order to convince you?"

Somehow the chill that had surrounded Alison seemed to be abating. "You want to marry me? But you never said anything . . ."

"How could I talk about marriage to you? That hotel was always between us like some impregnable fortress." He dropped his hands from her shoulders. "But I'm still going to build it. You've been wrong, Alison. Stubborn and bullheaded. Fairfax is going to have that resort—even if it means the end of us."

Alison looked into his haggard face and all the love she felt for him seemed to rush through her like a warm tide. "I've changed my mind," she said softly.

He looked down at her uncertainly. "You have?"

Her voice became stronger. "I've changed my mind about the resort. You were right about Fairfax, but I never understood until I came back from Key West. The buildings all need renovating, business is terrible, and the young people are leaving in droves. I'm . . . I'm sorry about everything. I guess I was just afraid of anything new."

Matt's hand cupped her chin and raised her lowered head until their eyes locked. "Alison, I . . ." Another icy gust blew between them and she shivered inadvertently. "You're freezing!"

At her nod Matt swept her up into his arms and walked onto the front porch, where he kicked the door open with his foot, entered the house, and shut the door behind him with his shoulder.

"Put me down," she insisted, half struggling and half laughing as he carried her over to the sofa. "This isn't a scene from a Victorian novel."

He grinned down at her in a way that made Alison's heart turn over. "Say yes and I'll let you go."

"Yes to what?" she asked in deceptive innocence, all the while reveling in the feel of his strong shoulder against her face.

"Yes, you'll marry me," he growled. "I'm beginning to get the feeling that you enjoy getting proposed to."

"I can't answer until I ask some questions," she teased.

He murmured something about how no one had ever told him how difficult a proposal could be, dumped her unceremoniously on the couch, and pulled off his jacket. "Okay," he said, sitting down beside her and pulling her close to him. "How many?"

"Four."

"I guess I can wait that long," he said in a lazy voice full of such a sensual warmth that Alison's cheeks turned pinker than they already were due to the cold. "What about Melissa?"

Matt looked astounded. "Melissa? Her father asked me to hire her to keep her out of trouble; she had gotten in with a rowdy crowd and needed something useful to do." He looked into Alison's face with perplexity. "What on earth do you think I'd want to do with Melissa?"

Alison thought it prudent not to enlighten him. "And Terry?"

A look of comprehension dawned in Matt's eyes. "My secretary?"

Alison nodded.

"Terry is engaged to a very nice law student."

"And Danielle?"

"You have quite an imagination," he said dryly. "Danielle was my mother's best friend. She helped bring me up." He paused. "Any more?"

Matt looked into the fire before answering the question in Alison's eyes. "Deanna and I had a thing going about five years ago. It was short-lived, but she never wanted it to end." He turned to Alison, and deep lights glinted in his eyes. "And I never wanted her the way I've wanted you."

Then he proved just how much by enfolding her in his arms and kissing her, at first gently and then very seriously, very deeply, and very passionately.

"Do I take it that your answer is yes?" Matt murmured minutes later, his lips moving against her hair.

"Yes." Alison sighed in contentment and wrapped her arms around his waist.

"I had intended to make a more formal proposal of marriage to you after the party, but you didn't give me a chance." He nibbled on her earlobe.

"I ran away."

"And I went crazy looking for you. Then Elizabeth collapsed and we had to rush her to the hospital."

Alison pulled away from him. "Matt! Is she all right?"

He ran a hand wearily over his eyes. "She had a mild heart attack, but I spent four days at the hospital with her until I was convinced that she would be fine. Actually"—and he grinned at the memory—"she told me to get out and go to Fairfax. She was afraid that you might be feeling neglected."

Alison snuggled back into his arms. "Abandoned was more like it."

"So I drove here in two straight days. I must have broken some kind of record."

"You look exhausted." She traced the deep lines around his mouth with her forefinger.

He kissed the tip of her finger. "How would you like to be in charge of the planning for the hotel."

"What?"

"After we're married, you can supervise the arrangements."

"But I don't know anything about hotel management!"

"You'll learn. I can't see you spending the rest of your life sitting by a swimming pool. You're too much of a fighter, Alison. I want us to work together."

Alison looked into the glowing embers of the fire. She hadn't thought about anything beyond Matt's proposal, but of course marriage to him would mean leaving Fairfax, her friends, and her job at the radio station. She felt saddened and yet exhilarated. Working with Matt would be a challenge, exhausting, demanding, and yet very fulfilling. And if there were children . . . ? Alison blushed but smiled contentedly to herself. There was nothing she wanted more in this world than to have Matt's children.

Alison looked up into Matt's eyes. "I love you," she whispered.

Matt's finger caressed the hollow of her throat. "I love you, too, Miss Alison Ramsey of Fairfax, New York." And then his mouth moved sensually against hers.

Samson leaped up onto the ottoman by the rocking chair and, for a few seconds, stared at Alison and Matt while licking a paw and running it over the tip of one furry ear. Then he turned around three times and, with a contented purr, lay down, tucking his paws under his chin and wrapping his tail over his nose.

In the silence, the fire crackled and popped as flames

danced around the logs and sent an orange glow into the room. A sudden shower of yellow sparks caused Alison to look around, but Matt pulled her firmly back into his arms. Then, reaching up with one hand, he pulled the cord on the table lamp and the fire glowed on into the darkness.

IT'S YOUR OWN SPECIAL TIME

Contemporary romances for today's women.

Each month, six very special love stories will be yours

from SILHOUETTE.

Look for them wherever books are sold

or order now from the coupon below.

$1.50 each

Silhouette Romance

___ #55 WINTER'S HEART Ladame
___ #56 RISING STAR Trent
___ #57 TO TRUST TOMORROW John
___ #58 LONG WINTER'S NIGHT Stanford
___ #59 KISSED BY MOONLIGHT Vernon
___ #60 GREEN PARADISE Hill
___ #61 WHISPER MY NAME Michaels
___ #62 STAND-IN BRIDE Halston
___ #63 SNOWFLAKES IN THE SUN Brent
___ #64 SHADOW OF APOLLO Hampson
___ #65 A TOUCH OF MAGIC Hunter
___ #66 PROMISES FROM THE PAST Vitek
___ #67 ISLAND CONQUEST Hastings
___ #68 THE MARRIAGE BARGAIN Scott
___ #69 WEST OF THE MOON St. George
___ #70 MADE FOR EACH OTHER Afton Bonds
___ #71 A SECOND CHANCE ON LOVE Ripy
___ #72 ANGRY LOVER Beckman
___ #73 WREN OF PARADISE Browning
___ #74 WINTER DREAMS Trent
___ #75 DIVIDE THE WIND Carroll
___ #76 BURNING MEMORIES Hardy

___ #77 SECRET MARRIAGE Cork
___ #78 DOUBLE OR NOTHING Oliver
___ #79 TO START AGAIN Halldorson
___ #80 WONDER AND WILD DESIRE Stephens
___ #81 IRISH THOROUGHBRED Roberts
___ #82 THE HOSTAGE BRIDE Dailey
___ #83 LOVE LEGACY Halston
___ #84 VEIL OF GOLD Vitek
___ #85 OUTBACK SUMMER John
___ #86 THE MOTH AND THE FLAME Adams
___ #87 BEYOND TOMORROW Michaels
___ #88 AND THEN CAME DAWN Stanford
___ #89 A PASSIONATE BUSINESS James
___ #90 WILD LADY Major
___ #91 WRITTEN IN THE STARS Hunter
___ #92 DESERT DEVIL McKay
___ #93 EAST OF TODAY Browning
___ #94 ENCHANTMENT Hampson
___ #95 FOURTEEN KARAT BEAUTY Wisdom
___ #96 LOVE'S TREACHEROUS JOURNEY Beckman
___ #97 WANDERER'S DREAM Clay
___ #98 MIDNIGHT WINE St. George
___ #99 TO HAVE, TO HOLD Camp

Silhouette **Romance**

15-Day Free Trial Offer
6 Silhouette Romances

6 Silhouette Romances, free for 15 days! We'll send you 6 new Silhouette Romances to keep for 15 days, absolutely free! If you decide not to keep them, send them back to us. You pay nothing.

Free Home Delivery. But if you enjoy them as much as we think you will, keep them by paying the invoice enclosed with your free trial shipment. We'll pay all shipping and handling charges. You get the convenience of Home Delivery and we pay the postage and handling charge each month.

Don't miss a copy. The Silhouette Book Club is the way to make sure you'll be able to receive every new romance we publish before they're sold out. There is no minimum number of books to buy and you can cancel at any time.

This offer expires February 28, 1982

Silhouette Book Club, Dept. **SBG**17B
120 Brighton Road, Clifton, NJ 07012

   Please send me 6 Silhouette Romances to keep for 15 days, absolutely free. I understand I am not obligated to join the Silhouette Book Club unless I decide to keep them.

NAME_____

ADDRESS_____

CITY_____ STATE_____ ZIP_____